# THE LADIES OF THE
# LORDLEIGH CLUB

In this his tenth and sexiest novel, Shepherd Mead reveals the intimate love-lives of the richest and most elegant ladies in some very, very posh club. Mead says, 'Making love is delightful, but it's only a charade without *liking*. And an *affaire* without wit is like a day without sunshine.' Did he actually *know* the likes of *The Ladies of the Lordleigh Club*? Where did he find Tish, a real Lady who climbed almost to the very top by slapping the right man in the right place? Or golden brown Lulu, who knew that the mud beside the yacht club was magically *alive*? Was Mead really Jo-Jo, the old roué of Lordleigh? The only way to find out is to read the book!

*By the same author*

How to Succeed in Business Without Really Trying
How to Live like a Lord Without Really Trying
The Admen

# The Ladies of the Lordleigh Club

*(and their incredible demands)*

SHEPHERD MEAD

ROBERT HALE · LONDON

© Shepherd Mead 1991
First published in Great Britain 1991

ISBN 0 7090 4529 8

Robert Hale Limited
Clerkenwell House
Clerkenwell Green
London EC1R 0HT

Photoset in North Wales by
Derek Doyle & Associates, Mold, Clwyd.
Printed in Great Britain by
St Edmundsbury Press, Bury St Edmunds, Suffolk.
Bound by WBC Bookbinders Ltd, Bridgend, Glamorgan.

# One

It was the year that Lordleigh came unstuck. It was the year they found Ferraris in the bushes and gorgeous studs on the tennis courts. It was the year when every woman at Lordleigh felt she might be under attack, and wondered whether she wanted to be – or not. It was the year when I felt I was, somehow, Horatio at the bridge, or all seven Samurai in one. Was there anything I could do to save the Lordleigh Club? How far could I go?

'What is Lordleigh?' you say, if you're a real Yank, and not a misplaced Yank, like me, but a real Yankee Doodle Dandy, the way I used to be. In that case you'd probably pronounce it 'Lordly', and not correctly, 'Lord-luh', swallowing the second syllable. Remember these British are people who pronounce Beaulieu as 'Bew-ly'. Around here, don't ever pronounce anything the way it's spelled.

But an English gentleman would *never* say, 'What is Lordleigh?' Well, no more than he would say, 'Who is the Queen?' or 'What is a pound?' The Lordleigh Club is a *tennis club*? Surely you're joking. They were playing *whist* at Lordleigh before tennis was invented, as well as cricket, and fives, and debating whether they should take up pig-sticking. But tennis is catching on. We now have forty-five courts, and with the new Aussie rubber

5

ones they're putting in, five different surfaces, including, of course the most beautiful grass in the world. Some say you could even *eat* it, with a bit of salad cream.

Everyone who is absolutely *anyone* belongs to Lordleigh, and the thousands who would mortgage their wives to get in simply don't have a prayer. Five-year waiting list. Could Lordleigh come crashing, and disintegrate into little sticky bits? More likely that Admiral Nelson would leap off his column in Trafalgar Square. That's what they'd have said before all this happened.

When did the crisis start? Well, the underlying rot must have begun long before, and surely I was part of the rotting, one of the softest apples in the barrel. But I think of my part as really dating from the time I was thrown into the Miss-Willy-four with Jamie.

Miss Willoughby-Fanning, usually called Miss Willy, was the match secretary. She had once reached the last thirty-two at Wimbledon, back when we were children. If you hadn't made up your own four, you signed with her and if you were one of 'Miss Willy's people' and occasionally gave her a bottle of Scotch, you were assigned to the better courts, and people who played a *useful* game.

I appeared at Miss Willy's counter in the Tennis Pavilion, dressed properly in whites, and bearing a racket and sufficient change to rent a quarter of the can of new yellow balls.

There were about a dozen others engaged in a terribly well-mannered milling about at the counter, just as the 2.30 session was forming up. Miss Willy, who was a snob, spotted Bunky Billcross in the second row, and said, 'Oh, Lord Billcross, you're on seven. They have balls already.'

'Thank you, Miss Willy,' said Bunky, with a slight stammer, and flushing a bit. This sort of red-carpeting embarrassed him, but it would have embarrassed him more to tell her to stop it.

Miss Willy got to me just about three and a half minutes before the one o'clock people had to get off the court, making it necessary to lope down past the tea lawn to Court Twenty-three, red shale, almost as far down as the stables. We would be a mixed, and the other three were waiting. I knew Alex already, a handsome stockbroker, like an older brother of a yuppy, who hit everything with all his might, and Laura, skinny, with lots of chop shots. It used to be Mister this and Miss that, but now it's all first names, and sometimes you don't even *know* the last name.

But the fourth was Jamie. I had *never* seen her as one of Miss Willy's sign-up people, but I knew her. Everyone knew Jamie. I had played against her before, mostly in mixed doubles tournaments.

But most important was the fact that Jamie was one of the ladies who, in effect, owned the Club. I'll tell you more about that later. She was dressed very informally. White, of course, but just a Fred Perry cotton-knit shirt, probably one of poor dear Alastaire's, but shaped as only Jamie could shape it, and shorts, long shorts, very rare for a female at Lordleigh, except for one like Jamie who didn't have to give a damn.

'Hello, Jo-Jo. You're getting fatter, aren't you?' I had given up trying to get Lordleigh women to call me Joe, or Joseph, and not Jo-Jo. Proving, I suppose that I would never live it all down. Women never forget.

'Not really, Jamie. I didn't know you were one of Miss Willy's people.'

'Anyone can be one of Miss Willy's people. How shall we play?'

Alex said, a bit too quickly, 'Why don't we take them on, Jamie?'

Jamie said, 'Let's flip rackets.' And after a bit of flipping which no one but Jamie understood, I wound up as her partner. I suspected she must have had some reason.

English women are almost always better tennis players than English men, because they play it at school as a sport, while their brothers are wasting their time on cricket. Jamie took the left-hand court without even asking, and with her beautiful topspin backhand, it was no problem. We won easily. She always did. It was the second reason she became poor Alastaire's second wife, to be his partner in the mixed. She used to play the left side with him, too. I wonder if she played the left side of the bed, as well.

As we were zipping up our racket cases, and after Alex and Laura had walked out, she said, 'I wonder if you'd mind helping me, Jo-Jo.' I had thought something was up. Jamie never did anything by accident.

'Yes, of course.'

'I need a strong arm to get a sun-dial into the car.'

We walked to one of the parking places, back near the cricket ground.

'Here we are,' she said. Anyone would have expected Jamie to be driving a Merc or a big BMW, but this was a Morris Minor wagon, which hadn't been made since early MacMillan, and cost new about £450. They went out when the Mini came in. But it was shiny, and in mint condition. Kind of a cult, like the old Model A Fords in the States.

We drove to one of those up-market garden furniture places, not the plastic gnomes, but the white concrete Rodins and the white-painted cast-iron chairs, Louis Quinze shape. She found the sun-dial, just the bronzy part you put on top.

'Oh, I'm sorry. I remembered it was bigger than that. You didn't really *have* to come.'

And she could have got the assistant to load it into the car, too, but that wasn't the point, was it?

'That would have been a pity,' I said.

'Yes, wouldn't it? Now I'll have to give you tea.' She was smiling sweetly. 'It isn't far, just this side of Sandown.'

'I remember,' I said.

'Oh yes, of course. How could I forget?' How, indeed.

We were in London commuter country, south-west, in Surrey, often called in the tabloid papers 'the stockbroker belt', though Alex was actually the only stockbroker I knew. Most people took the train to Waterloo.

Jamie drove through the gate and up the avenue of trees to Beech Holme and into the garage, next to the Bentley, which poor Alastaire would never drive again. The house, which must have had about a dozen bedrooms upstairs, was red brick and red tiles, with lots of gables, circa 1914. After Alastaire had flown, Jamie had the first and second floors made into three flats, which she rented, and had the whole ground floor done over for herself.

We walked in, and the maid, who must have heard the car, hurried to the door.

'We'll have tea on the terrace, Mrs Bolton.'

'Yes, ma'am.' Mrs B. was fortyish, plump, with a barely detectable cockney accent. Most people now had only cleaning women, called 'dailies', but even Jamie was down to a couple.

We walked in past the fine eighteenth century drawing-room, and Alastaire's billiard room, which she had left as it was, and directly to Jamie's bedroom. She had converted it from the large terrace room, with French doors leading directly on to the terrace. It was the biggest bedroom of my travelogue, and the bed was at least up to my average, a veritable playing-field.

'Remember, Jo-Jo?'

'Remember what, Jamie?'

The bathroom was gorgeous, too. She had done it all in marble, with the best stall shower in England.

We were in the bedroom only because the table was just outside, under a beach umbrella. Mrs B. brought the tea and scones. We were overlooking the lawn, almost an acre of it, with flower borders. The azaleas were in bloom and the rhododendrons were not quite ready. Bolton was snipping the dead-heads from the rose-bushes. The people in the upstairs flats had their own area. This was all Jamie's. Closer to us, on the little brick rim of the terrace, were concrete goblets about two feet high, full of geraniums.

'Well, you could hardly say it was an *affaire* that we had, Jo-Jo, more of a bash. I had to try you on, after all I'd heard.'

'Lovely, Jamie, stopping was your idea.'

'I wasn't sure I *liked* you, only what you did. And I was afraid I might become addicted. You were definitely addictive.'

'But what a pretty way to put it.'

'You did come on with a rush. But that's American, isn't it? No Englishman would plunge in that way.'

'No? How many chaps do you base that on, Jamie?'

'Stop it.'

'Are all the fellows just slightly afraid of women?'

'Well, they're not so pushy. They do go off and huddle with each other. They don't head for the ladies the way you do.'

'So that's true of all Yanks?'

'How can I be sure? You're the only Yank I ever slept with. I'm not the only native girl for you, am I?'

'Why did you bribe Miss Willy to get into my four?'

'You're changing the subject.'

'Yes, darling.'

'Well, *darling*, I didn't bribe her. I asked her.'

'You must be the only member who can do that.'

'There are at least half-a-dozen others who can actually *order* it, and be sure it's done.'

'All of them women?'

'Most of them. I wanted to talk to you. I thought you might be useful. And now I wonder. Have you gone off the boil?'

'Completely.'

'I must say you don't *seem* as sexy. Should we nip into the bedroom and do a sort of litmus test?'

'No.'

'I don't mean the whole bit. I could easily tell from one – well, one kiss. Not a peck, but one of your normals, down to the epiglottis, darling. That would show me, and I won't *allow* you to go an inch farther.'

'Any farther and you might digest me. I kiss only hands now, Jamie. Not a nibble above the wrist.'

'That wouldn't prove *anything*.'

'Lovely tea.' (The scones had been very nice.) 'May I go home now? Bolton and the Bentley, not your banger.'

'You mean you have really given up women? *You?*'

I stood up.

'Sit down, Jo-Jo!'

I stayed standing up.

'Listen to me, darling. Something very *sinister* is going on, and it must have something dangerous to do with the Club.'

'Oh?' I sat down.

'Have another cup of tea. I'm not through with you.'

'You've got the wrong man. I'm no sinister-fixer.'

'But it has clearly got something to do with sex. That's why I come to you.'

'Circumstantial evidence. *What* evidence?'

'There was a Ferrari parked in front of Fiona's house.'

'No one has ever become pregnant from a Ferrari. Little Ferraris?'

'But Fiona doesn't know any Ferraris. If she did I'd have heard about it. And I know the only two Ferraris at the Club. And one of them is fat. Then I saw Fiona playing singles with a man, on the Number Eleven grass court, the woodsy one that is almost private. I couldn't help sneaking behind one of the rhododendrons. He was *beautiful*. Tall, blond, rippling muscles. Definitely not a Club member. And only a tennis bum can play like that.'

'A tennis bum with a Ferrari?'

'Sinister, isn't it? And later I saw the two of them *in the Ferrari*, driving out on the Club road. Fiona definitely tried not to notice me. And two days later I saw Deirdre, being driven down the King's Road in a Lamborghini, and I don't know a *single* Lamborghini, they're practically extinct. The traffic was moving very slowly so I got a good view. He could only be a gigolo, wavy chestnut hair and a classical Greek profile. Simply good enough to *eat*.'

'Gigolos don't drive Lamborghinis.'

'That's exactly what I mean. Sinister. Somebody is

sending in the studs, the professional studs, not amateurs like you, Jo-Jo. What do Fiona and Deirdre have in common?'

'They're both sexy, they're both good tennis players. Like you. But neither one is likely to turn pro, either one way or the other.'

'You might say we all have. We all become the second wives, and mixed doubles partners of well-heeled Lordleigh leaders, old enough to be our fathers and all of them are now dead, so all of us are rich. The Club is what somebody is after. And maybe I'm next. You're simply going to have to put off becoming a eunuch, Jo-Jo. I thought of you somehow, in this situation as a *samurai*.'

'Isn't *samurai* plural?'

'The cavalry. The last shoot-out of the shot-up gunslinger.'

It's sad what American television has done to the English upper classes. Even the lower ones.

'Could you put that into English? British English? I can't bear American slang,' I said, in my most polished mid-western twang.

'You can't wriggle out of it, Jo-Jo. We need a Don Giovanni for this, but you're the best we've got.'

'The poor man's gun-slinging *samurai* satyr-eunuch? How can that possibly save the Club?'

'I don't know, but the first thing you can do is find out what they're after.'

'Just your money?'

'It must be more sinister than that. We've had the money for years. And if it's just money, they'd go first to Tish. I think she could buy us all out.'

'And they haven't?'

'If they have, we might not hear. Tish has ways of

stopping talk. And they might be afraid of what she'd do. Don't look so sad, Jo-Jo. Haven't you heard of rationalization? It may give you an excuse to go back to doing what you really like to do so well. I'll shout to Bolton. He can take you back in the other car.'

# *Two*

Amazingly, Bolton still remembered where I lived, and there was a bit of Bourbon in the Bentley's little bar. I considered it one of my finest achievements to have weaned Jamie away from Scotch, and obviously the wean still held. After Jamie's painful whipping I needed something stronger than tea.

We pulled up through my avenue of poplars and around the little pond with the Chinese ornament, a rather more impressive façade than Jamie's, in fact. The only difference was that my flat was just one of the little ones that Lady Richey had made out of her upstairs bedrooms. It suited me perfectly, my own entrance, and my own stairs – once servants' stairs – and we were right next to the Club. I had a pretty view of the Lordleigh lagoon, and some of the grass courts. My guests could simply fade away, behind the practice wall, and – presto! Who was to know where they – or she – had gone? Madeleine Richey would simply do *anything* for me and had got to the age where I didn't really have to do anything important for her except fill in a hole in a dinner party, or squire her to some Club Do. But she was always warm and *simpatica*. Old lovers make the best friends.

I saw her coming around from the main garden,

holding a secateur, British for clippers, one of those Wilkinsons that let you nip off the dead rose with one hand and drop it into the basket. The basket was half-full of dead roses. Bolton, as he drove off, must have noted that his mistress *never* had to do things like *that*.

'You need any help with that, Madeleine?'

'No, thank you, Joseph. Just stand there a moment, my dear, and let me look at you.'

I stood there and let her look at me, up and down. And while she was doing that, I couldn't help looking at her. Madeleine was still quite pretty, but she'd gone a bit plump. Legs still good, they usually last for years.

'Eerie, isn't it?' she said. 'He's still there.' The ladies used to claim I looked exactly like Cary Grant, as he was in his prime. I couldn't see it, but they all did. Wishful thinking, of course. Hallucination. They said I *was* Grant until I opened my mouth and Missouri came out. At forty-nine, I was grey at the temples. At least I was about Grant-size.

'You look all right, do you feel all right, Joseph?'

'Yes, dammit, I'm not sick. I've just been playing tennis.'

'I can see that. Come here and sit down.'

We were close to a teak settee that was surrounded by a large clump of honeysuckle. I sat down. This was my day for sitting down, under orders. The scent was practically an aphrodisiac.

'You can tell *me*.'

'What?'

'Joseph, I know you very well. Very. And I am still so fond of you. Really, it isn't as bad as you think.'

'No?' What wasn't?

'I've been talking with Marian, and she just let it slip. I

am so sorry for you. But it needn't be the end of everything. I remember when it happened to Bertie.'

Bertie, Sir Albert, bless his soul, had been her husband, one of my men's four, once, and I recall the time when he told me, in the Club Bar, 'No, God dammit, I *can't* any more!' He had been drinking a lot, and that sometimes removed the starch, leaving you limp or, as the British would say, 'Leaving one limp'. Madeleine was quite lovely then, fantastic breasts, and I never took a step in her direction, firm rule with wives of friends. Until Bertie was gone, of course, and then we did have a really memorable *affaire*. Is that what Marian said was wrong with me? Did she think I'd gone limp? It was certainly not based on any actual encounter. Marian and I hadn't, for years. And I was perfectly OK – well, then at least.

'No, don't give up, Joseph. You *can* make adjustments. Do you need instruction, my dear? I'd be glad to do *anything*. Some of the bits are quite delightful. After all, I think of you as – well, almost a natural resource.'

Now really, what words can you use to reassure a lovely lady on such a delicate point? No, Lady Richey, somebody has misinterpreted the facts? I am changing my way of life, but I *can* still get it up? I must have turned red, and spluttered.

'I don't know what Marian is talking about,' I said.

'Oh, I am sorry. I've embarrassed you, my dear. Forget I said anything. Did you have a nice game?'

'A dreadful game, Madeleine. I must go now, and change. I have to drive in to town. God bless.' I kissed her on the cheek, but affectionately, with a bit of a squeeze, and went upstairs.

I turned the Porsche toward London. I feel I have to apologize for it. Porsche has become almost a dirty word now. This was *not* a yuppy Porsche, it was an antique Porsche, fourteen years old, the way they used to make them, like a Beetle, with the motor in the back. They still make a few of these 911s for the Americans. I bought it when Gwenny and the kids and I had the big house with the acre of garden in St George's Hill. The Volvo wagon was for them. This was for me. Now they make suped up Volkses that can run rings around me, but I'm sentimental about it, and they last forever. Just remember, the back sometimes breaks away in the wet.

I'd think twice about driving into London on a weekday, but this was Sunday, and I knew several yellow-line places in Chelsea, near Subby's, where I could park. Subby is short for Sublimity, her mother's fault, she'd never have called herself that. There was no way I could have seen her at the club that afternoon. One of her authors was in town that weekend. But she knew I was coming.

I found a place just two blocks away and walked into her little dead-end mews, her own tiny house, a picturesque Georgian brick, probably made over from a stable, just three rooms and a walled garden. Mind you, outside the commuter range you could have bought a trout stream, a paddock, four acres and a five-bedroom stately home for the same money.

I had a key. When I opened the door, I heard a muffled shout from the bathroom. 'I'm running a bit late, darling. Walk slowly in this direction.' She almost galloped to meet me in a white terry bathrobe, befogged by a showery mist, no makeup, and wearing nothing else but mules. When she reached me, she flung the robe open, and the bare breasts, looking pink as though they had just been rubbed with a rough towel, pressed against me. That was Subby, tall, blonde, and normally looking (when properly dressed) very cool. Before she said a word she kissed me thoroughly.

'Darling,' she said, 'I've been waiting for you all day, and getting sexier and sexier. The cover is off the bed.' I knew the way. She helped me tear off my clothes. Subby liked you to *charge!* and then linger, lazily linger, for the longest possible time. And with kisses everywhere. But *everywhere*. It was a wonder we didn't burn each other down.

'Well now,' she said, 'what have you been up to?'

'You'll talk to me now?'

'If you promise not to be intelligent. She came *here*, she wanted to, after a hideously expensive lunch at the Connaught. She wanted to find out how we Briddish intellectuals lived. I have talked myself hoarse. She's off now. She'll be on Channel Four tomorrow telling all about her book, and then back to New York. Are you still a virgin?'

'No woman will touch me now. They're afraid I'm not old enough. I had a mixed four with Jamie. Tennis only. She thinks I won't, and Madeleine thinks I can't. See what you've done to me?'

'Well, maybe Madeleine is right.'

She expected a spank on the bare bottom for that, but not too hard, darling, just the right yummy-spank. It almost set us off again.

'Can you stand monogamy, lover?' she said.

'It depends on mono-who. Mono-you? Yes. Can you?'

'Yes, with you.'

'Absolute?'

'Absolute. These days it has to be absolute.'

We thought we'd try it, and see. Neither of us was

sure we wanted to be married again, but at the moment we were certainly in love.

'Have you seen any extra Ferraris around the Club, Subby?'

'I'm not there as much as you. Why?'

'Jamie thinks somebody is sending studs to attack the Lordleigh maidens.'

'Have they got as far as Jamie?'

'Not yet. One to Fiona, and a Lamborghini to Deirdre.'

'I thought Lamborghinis were gay. Maybe the ladies called *them*, themselves. Were they lonesome, with you in pasture? What about Tish?'

'I haven't heard. I'll bet they're afraid of Tish.'

'*You're* afraid of Tish.'

I said nothing to that.

'Well, anyway, *I'm* afraid of Tish, where you're concerned.'

Subby had an aunt who lived in Cobham. Sometimes she would stay with her over weekends, to be closer to the Club. She could easily sneak in to my flat, any time. She worked for a publisher in the West End. Few editors could live in her style in Chelsea, unless they'd bought before the inflation. But Subby was relatively rich. Her father, a wealthy city chap, had retired from the Stock Exchange to Guernsey, in the Channel Islands, with a lovely house in St Peter Port, so that Subby was able to inherit most of the money. She'd been divorced for about six years.

Since it was Sunday evening, there was something terribly cultural on the box, I forget what. We thought we'd have a look while we recharged our batteries. I reckoned I had better not mention Jamie's plans for me. Not that I had the slightest intention of leaving my virtuous and exclusive position, to go sliding back into the gilded fleshpots of the Lordleigh Club. My way would be the clean-living way; more jogging, more virtue all around, and violent, monogamous sex with Subby. Couldn't wait, in fact, for the second round.

# Three

At Rambleys it was an unwritten rule that no meetings were ever held before noon on Monday, so the people could come in from their cottages in Hampshire, or their yachts on the Solent, and avoid the ten-mile tailbacks on the motorways. This gave Subby and me a chance to sleep late, and renew our acquaintance, just a lovely, erotic snack, before breakfast. She was thrice-blessed, company-wise as well, having sacrificed almost a whole Sunday to literature. She'd just stay home and play with somebody's manuscript.

After lunch I took the car to the basement parking of the agency, up near Holborn. It was, in fact, considered by the accountants to be one of their cars, or, a company car, like everybody else's, meaning they paid all the expenses on it. Imagine *that* on Madison Avenue.

I went straight to the screening room. That's where a lot of my consulting took place. They say old admen in New York never die, they go to London to consult. 'Old' in New York advertising is anything over thirty-five. The slower pace suits their slight deceleration.

My specialty had always been TV advertising, and in the early days of British commercial television we Yanks were supposed to know more about it. I can tell you now, the limeys have caught up. Max was already there.

He had to be, because he worked for the film production house, and we at the agency, at Rambleys, were the customers. Max was bald and fat, and much shorter than I was, so we made a strange-looking couple, but our brains were synchronized: somehow, we thought in tandem. We were more than the sum of our parts. After being thrown together by business, in animated cartoon commercials, we started doodling around, also in animation, just for fun. It had nothing to do with advertising, and was totally different stuff.

I did most of the words and the basic ideas, and Max was a genius with a sketch-pad and a story-board, and a real pro with the mind-boggling technology of animation. We shared the serious animator's nausea about Disney-Cute, but we had no illusions commercially. With the box-watchers, Disney style had won completely. Every frame had to be fighting cute.

In fact the two of us were responsible for the cutest, cunningest little darling in British advertising, the Chocky Beans Sweety Bear, a cuddly teddy bear come to life, cute enough to make you throw up. I was consulting on the chocolate beans account, and had the idea. I wrote the words to the jingle, and suggested the artwork to Max, who took it and ran with it beautifully, and styled the whole animation as only Max could. Sort of kiddy-caviar with chocolate sauce. It was how we got to know each other. We shared the guilt.

The Chocky Bear is better known now than certain Royals, and most of the members of the cabinet. The jingle is whistled more often than 'Pomp and Circumstance' and 'God Save the Queen' put together. They have tripled the sale of, forgive me, Chocky Beans, and helped make the British the world record-holders for false teeth.

'How did it go, Max?'

'The boys and girls were at it most of the weekend.'

'Sorry about that.'

'Well, the Chairman said he wanted it more lovable. More like his own wittle teddy bear.'

'Is it?'

'Definitely. But only you and I can tell the difference in a pencil test.'

'The Chairman is supposed to come to this.'

(Whisper.) 'Oh, God.'

(Whisper.) 'I know.'

Cedric, the account manager, slipped in. 'I heard that,' he said.

'So blackmail us,' I said. I had known Cedric for years, and knew how he suffered. He was on our side.

'He's here, so it won't be long.'

He arrived, grey sideburns, florid complexion, Savile Row suit. Everybody stood up. The Chairman expected everyone to stand up when he entered a room.

'Let's see it,' he said and sat down in the front row of the two in the small room. Then we all sat down. Lights were dimmed, screen was lit up, showing a white background with messy pencil lines moving in synch with the Chocky Beans jingle. It was a very rough sketch of the bear, being lovable, and having a cutey-pants castrato orgasm over chocolate beans. The object was to show exactly, to the twenty-fourth of a second, which frame flashed in time with the sound track, which had been recorded first of all.

The Chairman said, 'I don't like that word yummy.'

There was a total silence. All of us knew that this comment threw us back to square one. Yummy was there because it rhymed with tummy, and that couplet, one of dozens I had written, a word I use loosely, had risen to the top in the fifth or sixth meeting with the Rambleys creative group, had survived three meetings with the client, was mortally wounded in the seventh client meeting, but revived in the eighth. The chairman had seen it in a dozen different scripts and five story-boards. No matter, his word was gospel, or sentence of death, to the fifth power. Changing the word would mean, first, a new couplet, several more client meetings, three or four more story-boards, and finally a new recording session, and a whole different pencil test, even if the change made a difference of only a tenth of a second.

'Surely,' said the Chairman, 'this whole Mickey Mouse department can think up another word. Let me know how you manage. Good day, gentlemen.' He stood up and walked out, not even giving us time to stand up.

We three just looked at each other.

Cedric said, 'Remember, fellows, we are paid by the week, and not by the piece.'

'I'm not,' said Max.

'We'll renegotiate the contract, Max,' said Cedric. 'He's basically a print man. He's never been happy since eighty per cent of the budget went into Chocky Bears. Let me know when you find a new line, Joseph, and we'll rev up the cuddly circus again. Cheers.' He left.

The change might cost fifty thousand pounds or so, but I knew that the Chairman was not worried about the money. Rambleys were already rotating six Bear spots several times a week on Channels Three and Four, and taking fifteen per cent of the air time, which varied, but came as high as thirty or forty thousand pounds a shot. This would be Bear Number Seven, and of the extra production cost Rambleys would get their usual fifteen per cent as well.

Max said, 'Come on back to the shop with me. I've changed the story-board on the middle section.'

We were actually trying to write and design a feature-length animated film, on our own. It could take years, and the odds against production, at a cost of millions, were astronomical, but we were having fun, and it helped to keep the chocolate out of our hair.

After looking at Max's new ideas, I dribbled in a few words, subject to a thorough pushing around on my processor. Then I walked back to Rambleys' underground garage. It was almost four, which was as late as you dared to start if you wanted to reach home before bed-time. My ageing chariot could do better than 110, but the average in London, even before the rush hour, was about eight miles an hour.

Madeleine waved to me as I pulled into her driveway. I waved back and blew her a kiss. But I kept on going. Never let a woman get started, unless you want to stay. I parked beside my entrance and hurried up the stairs. I wanted to get rid of this headful of broken eggs before they got scrambled, and the Macintosh was the only way.

First I brewed up a pint mug of Marks and Spencer's Extra Strong Tea, with two bags, strong enough to eat with a knife and fork. When you start doing that you have become, as my Yank friends would say, rilly Briddish.

It's blacker than black coffee, with three times the horsepower, and half the knock. I had become, like so many English people, a tea addict, especially when I wanted to work. Tea at this strength is not as powerful as speed, but close, and speed, even the simple pills, is now criminal, and a good thing, too. I squeezed a quarter of a lemon into it. No sugar.

Then I went into Macintosh's tiny room, not much bigger than a closet (a word meaningless to the British, except when preceded by the word *water*). It was filled with filing cabinets, a bookcase that went up to the ceiling, and a reclining chair right beside the computer, which was on a swivel, so it could be swung over close to me. I sat in the chair, put my feet up, pulled a bedside table over my lap, put my keyboard and the Mac and mouse on it, and swung the Mac over so that the screen was about a foot and a half from my myopic eyes. In other words, I was lying down. Keep the body relaxed and the mind alert. The main danger here is going to sleep.

The Rambleys problem, which required no real thought, could wait. Max's problem, which could blow your brain, needed instant attention. Our whole story-board, about fifty pages of it, was on my hard disk, and I punched it up on to the screen, then flipped to this afternoon's section. I wiped out the old line, typed in the new one I had suggested, then inserted that into the place on the story-board, and that set me off on a new idea. The whole thing was changing in front of my eyes. After typewriters this is a whole different world. For half an hour – or was it an hour? – time has a spooky new dimension when the words are flashing like pocket lightning through microchips; I was absorbed. When I had something that looked good, I punched the *save* button. I would look at the whole new bit in the morning, and then maybe throw it all out. The parts that still looked good I would copy on to a floppy disk in half a minute and send it by my modem, over the phone line, to Max's Mac in town, in a nanosecond. End of intelligent work.

Then I flipped to the *Chocky* document where I had

dozens of old Bear lyrics, and began a memo which would go to half-a-dozen Rambley people on the Beans account. 'Bear with me, fellows, while we reconsider the script of Bear Number Seven.' This required no actual writing, just *cutting* and *pasting* electronically, showing them the current words 'chosen for revision', no mention of the fact that the Chairman had thrown them out, and presenting seven or eight alternatives, with enough word changes to make them look just different enough. When printed it would fill three or four pages, enough to give the creative group plenty of fodder for five or six meetings. And at the end I threw them a few eager and optimistic exhortations from my list of eager and optimistic exhortations, just as though it all really mattered. Anyone reading this compilation would be sure that a New Start was under way and that I was in control of the whole situation, and worth all that money they paid me.

I pressed the *print* button, and while it was doing the work, buzzing back and forth over the paper with perforated edges, I wandered over to the Club to see what was going on. This was one of those incredible English summer evenings when the dark doesn't come until about 10.30. Some people were still playing tennis, many of them in sweaters because of the cool breeze.

As I passed one of the grass courts on the edge of the woods someone in a mixed doubles tried to hit a topspin lob, and caught it with the edge of the racket. The ball rose into the sky, far over the nylon netting, and over my head into the thickest part of the woods. It was a notorious place for losing balls.

Somebody said, 'Forget it, Joe! You'll need a machete.'

'I think I see it.' It was a bright yellow ball, and just by luck I did spot it in the underbrush. I picked it out and threw it back over the netting. Squeals of joy.

'Oh, Jo-Jo I love you!'

'I love you, too, darling.' What *was* her name anyway? Frightful player. But she must have heard what they said about me, and women. Lies, some of them.

I kept going through the woods. And then the trees and bushes became too familiar. I had a sense of left-over sadness, of wanting almost to cry. I came to a thicket, and a small clearing, like a room built around a silver birch, with a smooth stone for sitting. It was what Gwenny called our woodsy nook, and it made Gwenny come flitting back like a swarm of cock-eyed fairies, all carrying horoscopes, and playing tag with the planetaries. Oh, Gwenny, Gwenny, Gwenny, long gone but still flapping about inside me.

In the last days of Gwenny, with Crandie grown up and gone away, she would come to the woodsy nook, to sit on the smooth stone, and listen to the twittering of birds, always hundreds at Lordleigh, mixed with the faraway squeals of tennis, and pretend we were very close, in a fairy-story way, though it was about the only way, in those late days, that we were close at all. I would be aching for Gwenny, as I always was, even then, and Gwenny was aching for nobody at all, nobody made of warm flesh. With Gwenny, then, there was only wispy affection, all dreamy software and no hardware at all.

'Remember when we were in love, Joey? Can you remember back then?'

And I'd say, 'I don't have to remember, Gwenny. I'm still in love with you, real gutsy love. You're still the most beautiful girl in the world.' This wasn't really true, she was almost as old as I was. But she had been the most beautiful girl in Wisconsin, to say nothing of several neighbouring states. And maybe the most beautiful legs in the whole lot of them, and they were still there, still long and gorgeous.

'Don't go back into all that, Joey, and don't squeeze me, we're beyond that part now.'

'You are, but I never will be, and that's our problem.'

# *Four*

So now I've done it, and we'll have to leave the *Rape of the Lordleigh Ladies* cooking on the back burner, while I explain it all, or you'll never believe how I, a nice, moral workadaddy, with a wife and kid, came to be the amateur champion stud of the Lordleigh Club. But it's true, really true, and I can prove it.

When I first met Gwenny it was evident she must have been the most beautiful girl in the state of Wisconsin. I say that even though I've never been there. Wisconsin came to me, swept over me, changed my whole life. This sometimes happens to lonely, impressionable young men who come to New York from Missouri. They are the victims of dastardly companions, sometimes from Wisconsin.

While I was fresh out of Washington University, in St Louis, carrying packages for a New York advertising agency. I found myself surrounded by a shifty-eyed group speaking with a Wisconsin accent, not an easy one to spot. One of them, named Charlie, was carrying packages for the same advertising agency that I was. He and two friends had just graduated from the University of Wisconsin and had come to New York. They had rented the cheapest two-bedroom apartment in Jackson Heights, a five cent subway-ride to Madison Avenue, and they were looking for one more member to spread the cost. They would try to forget I was from Missouri.

The leader of the pack was Roger, a couple of years older. He had been to New York for a year, and had returned to the university for his last year, to get his degree. When you arrive in New York from the Midwest, it is obvious that this is a different country. They even talk a different language. But it takes about a year to tell *how* different. Roger already knew. And he was the one who introduced me to Gwenny. If he had done it then, when I moved in, who knows what would have happened? I was not yet ready for Gwenny. If she had come then, I might have lost her.

My mother, a totally good woman, would have thought Roger was an evil man, because he was preoccupied with sex. As far as I was able to discover, my mother knew nothing about sex, had never even *heard* of it. She certainly never mentioned it to us, never even said the word out loud. I assumed my brothers and I must have been conceived by immaculate conception. Living at home made this even worse. I did, because our house was close to the campus.

The Club Wisconsin, Jackson Heights Division, was completely preoccupied with sex. I was, too, but I really did not know how to go about it. In St Louis you could go about it for a dollar, east of Grand Avenue, but you didn't have to persuade the ladies. It was pre-packaged and the whole process took about ten minutes. Almost like going to the toilet. I often wondered, is this all there is to it? When I entered the Club Wiss, I still didn't know how to persuade a lady to do it, free. The other fellows all seemed to know.

Roger asked me, 'Frankly, Joe, you're not queer are you?' The word 'gay' then just meant happy. Sad to lose such a nice word.

'Oh, gosh, no!'

'I mean, there's a lot of the real stuff around. Wouldn't you like a piece of it?'

'Oh, yeah.'

'I think you're just shy.'

'Yeah. Maybe.' I was very embarrassed.

'You need somebody at first to meet you half-way. Somebody a little older. Maybe hungrier. How about a motherly nymphomaniac?'

'Really?'

'I know one. She might even rape you. Would you like that?'

'Yes.'

'She's a nurse, and a drunk. Her name is Doreen. Bring her some booze. I'll give you her number. Have you got the guts to call her?'

At least I was curious. How in the world could a woman rape a man? I phoned her, and she certainly didn't sound fierce, only disappointed it wasn't Roger. But she said to come along. I bought two quarts of beer. If she was really a heavy drinker, I didn't want her to get too drunk too quickly, before the raping was over.

She lived on the upper west side of Manhattan, so I took the elevated and the subway. Her apartment was in an old brownstone. I rang her bell, and wondered if she would pounce on me. She opened the door and said, 'Hello, come in,' very quietly. The symphonic music of WQXR was playing softly. But I did notice she was in a negligée, the sort of thing a woman might wear for raping. My first thought was that she was not quite old enough to be my mother. Maybe she was thirty, which to me, then, at that age, was practically senile. She did have a pretty good figure. Her breasts, which were almost hanging out, were larger than average, and she had a slight resemblance to a bloodhound, that is, she was slightly jowly, but she was much prettier than an ordinary bloodhound.

Doreen sat on the studio couch, narrower than a double bed. I sat beside her, and left my bag of beer on the floor. She was making no threatening motions, in fact quite the opposite, she was looking at me in a kindly, and non-raping manner. I kissed her on the lips. I was quite a good kisser, because I had done a lot of necking, in the car, back home. I even went over to kissing her breasts, and I was OK at that, too. This made her breathe quite quickly, and she said, 'Why don't we take off our clothes?' I said OK, and we did.

I had a feeling she was waiting for me to lead, like in dancing, and I didn't know where to go from there. She just sort of snuggled, in an affectionate way, not attacking at all, and moved her legs slightly apart, inviting me in. In fact, she kind of helped me to get in. But very gently, and then did a lovely undulating movement. 'Don't try to hurry,' she said. 'The longer it takes, the better.'

But I did hurry, in spite of myself. 'Oops!' I said. And *Oooooops*! I did.

'Never mind,' she said. 'It will be better next time.'

Did she want me to leave? 'Do you have anything to do later this evening?' I asked.

'Not a thing. Just lie back.'

The symphony on WQXR kept on playing, and we talked, and drank some of the beer. She had come up to Manhattan from Tennessee, and she worked at Mt Sinai Hospital. She had had many lovers, including young doctors, who had taught her a great deal. She read the *New Yorker*, not just the cartoons, even the stories. We had that and the music in common.

I noticed that one of her legs happened to get between mine. It just rested there, without really moving, but I could feel the pulse. Pretty soon I thought more about that than anything. My enthusiasm was beginning to grow. She leaned over and kissed me, very gently but thoroughly and put her hand down and held me in a terribly loving way, and then just eased me in.

'Don't even move, darling, just throb,' she said.

'Yes, teacher.'

She did a lazy, voluptuous figure eight, which gave me the best feeling I ever had in my life. The second inning was certainly better. I had never played a second inning before.

'Now try it your way,' she said.

'I haven't got a way.'

'You will have, darling.'

And so began the Doreen lessons. I had no idea the subject was so complicated, or so fascinating, or so absolutely delicious. I didn't love Doreen, but I liked her very much, and I absolutely adored making love with her, but *really, seriously* making love with her. With Doreen it was an art, like playing the violin, or doing a *pas de deux*, or a conscientious topspin backhand, and make it last as long as possible. We always used condoms, which Roger and I used to buy by the gross, from a mail order place in Indiana.

I kept on coming to see Doreen two or three times every week for a whole year, and by that time Doreen had to admit she had taught me everything she knew. And the pretty young ladies who came to our parties at the Club Wiss could sense it, don't tell me how. One of them, named Lynn, was a tall and very well-shaped brunette, a divorcée. She had once ignored me completely. She looked at the new me and said, 'My, how you've changed!'

'How do you mean?' I asked.

'You know how I mean,' she said, and I could tell by the way she looked at me what she did mean. I had the confidence, and somehow it showed. One evening when I knew Doreen would be on duty, I called Lynn for a date, and before I knew it we were in bed, at her place. 'Where in the world did you learn all *that*?' she asked. I didn't say. The next time she invited me to dinner, a very nice dinner, just the two of us.

The same thing happened with two other Club Wiss ladies. Somehow the word had got around.

And so, without my knowing that Gwenny was coming. I was ready for her. When the next year's crop of Wisconsins came to New York she was with them. She was just in time for one of our big beer parties, with a quarter barrel, and lots of singing.

I had put down three or four glasses and sung the Whiffenpoof song at least twice when Gwenevere came in. She was not even *with* anybody, which was unbelievable for a girl who looked like that. Roger, our leader, had known her at Wisconsin, and asked her to come over for the party. She had been the Homecoming Game Girl, or something like that, and anyone could see why. Her hair was reddish-brown and she had the most beautiful legs I had ever seen, and everything else to match. Her eyes were large and green and the face was simply perfect. I said I was Launcelot's kid brother, Launcelittle, and that got us started. I was in love with her from that minute.

The men all flocked around Gwenny. With a girl who looked like that, they always did. I thought, well, there's no chance for me. But in the course of the big flurry, somehow we got to talking about birthdays, and I told her mine, April 26. The lovely big green eyes began to glow with what must surely have been an interplanetary gleam.

'Oh! You're a Taurus!' she said in an adoring tone, just as though it were an advantage.

'Is that good?' I had always assumed that astrology people were loony, but to Gwenny it was no joke.

'Not for everyone. The twenty-sixth, really? Are you sure?'

'I was too young at the time to read the calendar.'

'Oh, I can tell. You are.'

Roger, who overheard this, in passing, said, 'How lucky can you be?'

Gwenny said, 'Roger isn't a believer. Are you?'

'Not yet,' I said. I always claimed I didn't believe in belief. Either you knew, or you didn't. But Gwenny could have made me believe in Santa Claus. 'Enlighten me.'

'It isn't like fairy stories. It's scientific. It's based on the position of the planets. I'll work out your horoscope.' I was listening, but she could see where I was looking. 'It isn't down there.'

'Oh, sorry. You do have the loveliest legs I ever saw.'

'You have to be serious.'

'I'll try.'

I did try. Astrology is an industry the size of, maybe, plumbing plus pork bellies, and more books and columns have been written about it than about cholesterol. I explored it, as far as it went, and I still don't understand why the fact that the planets were doing whatever they were doing on that 26th of April made me the perfect mate for Gwenevere MacInnes, any more than anybody else born the same time. But she thought it did, and nothing else mattered.

Gwenny had a first-class brain, and a huge IQ, even so. It was something the psychologists would call a logic-tight compartment. Sometimes these viruses come down through their mothers. She had skipped grades, she had an 'A' average, and she was a superb cook. She was the perfect woman, except for that one thing, which I couldn't even guess at the beginning, and I was absolutely crazy in love for her.

I took her home by subway to her residence hotel that night, and kissed her once, standing up, before she went into the elevator, alone. No males were allowed above the ground floor. I was glad of that. Gwenny was too beautiful to be available to any male. Any other male, except me.

After that evening I never wanted any other girl but Gwenny, and it lasted for decades. She must have felt the same about me, and we were married within the year. Gwenny had no trouble finding a job, doing research for Time Inc. and I stopped carrying packages for the ad agency, and began my apprenticeship in the radio and television department. My salary rose gradually, every year. We started, at first, by renting a small 'studio' apartment in Jackson Heights, really just one room with a bathroom and a kitchenette on one wall. We could afford it, and we could commute for a five cents a ride.

At that time there was a famous head-hunter named Walter Lowen. If advertising agencies wanted an experienced copywriter or account man, they would go to Walter, and he would find somebody at another agency. Walter shifted me twice, and each time my salary was doubled.

After my first double, we moved to an apartment in Forest Hills with two bedrooms and a plastic waterfall in the back yard. Commuting by the new Eighth Avenue subway was even faster, and still cost five cents. Twelve minutes to Madison Avenue. Later, after another double, we moved farther out on Long Island, to a house on the North Shore.

Gwenny and I both wanted to have babies, and Crandie arrived as soon as possible.

Most men who make love regularly with a very beautiful woman, like Gwenny, will tell you this: yes, it is wonderful. It is the most wonderful thing in the world.

'But,' you might ask, 'did you ever make love, before that, with a woman not so beautiful?'

'Oh, yes.'

'No difference?'

'I'll take beauty every time. But of course you have to remember that a really gorgeous woman has a problem. Ever since she popped her first lovely breast, men have been the problem. They have always been after her, and with one thing in mind. She wishes, she desperately wishes, that they would please think about something else. Some begin to hate sex. Some even commit suicide to get away from it.'

This was no problem at all for Gwenny, at first. We did have lovely, affectionate mating for years. Of course she was choosey. She wouldn't do many things that Doreen or Lynn would do, and mouths were only for kissing other mouths. No matter, she was a fairy queen, and I loved her to pieces, and we made each other very sex-happy, with many celebrations. We intended to have at least three children and we kept right on trying. But all we had after Crandie were two miscarriages. Finally Gwenny was told she could never have any more.

By that time I was beginning to have power over women, like beautiful, charming copywriters for instance. I could have had anything I wanted. But with Gwenny, I was never even tempted.

Coming to England wasn't really my idea. The company was beefing up its London office. Would I like to go? It would probably be for two or three years, and then we could come back. Gwenny and I talked about it, and decided – yes.

We rented our Long Island house furnished, to people we knew, and flew to London. Our office was in Knightsbridge, in the south-western part of London, not far from Harrods. The company helped us to find a flat nearby.

Our problem was, we loved England, and we loved the English. We had a little trouble at first with the language. I mean, somebody might come at you with something like this: 'Smashing, Joseph! You hit it for six and Bob's your uncle! I bished mine, mucked up the lot, and won't get a quid for donkey's years.' (*Superb! You achieved the utmost, and are surely in an enviable position. I made a mess of mine and shall not receive even a pound in the foreseeable future.*) On the other hand, they will have no problem with your mother tongue, which they have been hearing for hours every week, from Dallas, Denver and points east. They simply think you are talking funny, like the telly. And they are ever so nice to you.

We decided to stay. The whole saga of our life in England, and how we came to live almost like lords, is another story, and one certainly worth telling. We discovered a beautiful but almost ruined house in a lovely part of Surrey called St George's Hill, bought it and made it actually liveable. And we managed to find

Crandie a place in the great, very private public school named Charterhouse, a few miles away. He was a boarder there from the time he was a beginning 'fag' at thirteen, until he was the head of his House at eighteen. Then he spent three years at Sussex University, down near the Channel. And after that he decided to go to the States. We joined both the St George's Hill Club and the Lordleigh Club. And I found my old friend Max in London, and we managed to make a big success with a silly little thing, so big that I left my old company, in a friendly way. It was all very happy, all except the part about Gwenny. She became ill, and less and less interested in anything physical. Finally she died.

I was thinking of things like that, a whole family ago, there in Gwenny's woodsy nook among the trees of the Lordleigh Club. The light was almost gone, and so was Gwenny, long gone.

I walked back to Madeleine's place, and up the servants' stairway. The little green lights on the Mac's printer were glowing in the darkened room, and so was the red light on the answerphone. Mac's three pages were all finished, and Jamie's voice, on tape, said: 'Where have you been, Jo-Jo? Please ring me right away.'

The live Jamie said, 'What steps have you taken, Jo-Jo?'

'None. It's no good pestering me, Jamie.'

'The situation is worse. They're closing in. I heard through Mrs Bolton that Joanna has been burgled.'

'What has that got to do with the rape of the Lordleigh maidens?'

'Only that somebody reported seeing an Aston in Joanna's rhododendrons.'

'Ridiculous. Burglars don't drive Astons.'

'That's the whole point, Jo-Jo.'

'What did they take?'

'Nobody could figure out what. I want you to go over to see her, first thing in the morning.'

'Joanna is part horse. She's all kitted out in boots and spurs and riding crops. She might saddle me for a canter and I wouldn't be able to sit down for a week.'

'I told her what you need is discipline. You're getting out of hand. She said she'd give you breakfast. 8.30 sharp.'

'I'll wear a bit in my teeth.'

# Five

I allowed half an hour. Joanna lived far from the Club, to the west. I drove out along the Hog's Back, with the green, rolling, Surrey Hills on both sides. The old car knew it well. I used to wander around this way years ago when Crandie was at Charterhouse, often picking him up for a home visit on Sundays. And because it was Joanna I was wearing jodhpurs, not that I really intended to use them.

I drove right up to the paddock, near the huge, part-ancient, half-timbered house and parked beside her Range Rover, which was still attached to her horse box. I was just standing up beside the car when Joanna, in jeans and riding boots, strode right up to me and kissed me firmly on the lips, warm, business-like, but no fooling around.

'Good to have you back, Jay-Jay, it's like old times. I see you're all ready to ride.'

'Just the uniform of the day, Annie. You know me, I'd be stiff for a week.'

'When you were around here, old dog, *I* was stiff for a week.' She gave me a squeeze. Not a come-on at all, a palsy squeeze, with a friendly smile.

'You were just used to the short sprints, Annie. No way to treat a good woman.'

Joanna was big, large breasts, slightly heavy legs, black curly hair. Impossible to explain Annie. She was the kindest of the women I knew, yet without an ounce of sentimentality. Doesn't add up, does it? She'd take a lot of trouble for anybody, almost as much as for a lover, and I don't think she had many more of those, after me. She was the one with the big money in that marriage. Her father had battled his way up with his own regional newspaper, practically printed it himself, and added one after another until he had millions. He was a great rider. The polo people said he'd have been the greatest if he'd had the time. She and Charles, usually called Cha-Cha, met on horses.

'What do you hear from Cha-Cha?' I asked. They'd been divorced for years.

'Saw him a few weeks ago at a point-to-point. He had a skinny blonde with him.'

'Poor girl.'

'Oh, I don't know. She was *clinging* to him. Looked happy. Cha-Cha is still very nice. And still beautiful, too.' (*Beautiful with a 't', English-style, always sounds so much prettier than bewdiful.*)

Annie had always had a no-nonsense view about sex. No mysteries, no la-de-dah, and it certainly wasn't *dirty*. Horses did it, too, didn't they? Could be a roaring good time and she was all for it, even though she had had the worst possible initiation to it. She used to talk about her sex with Cha-Cha while we were in bed together. He was a quick-bang man, sometimes six or seven times a day, anywhere, on the stairs, in the stable, bang-bang, and out. 'Didn't leave any time for celebrations, for me, if you know what I mean, Jay-Jay. Always plenty of celebrations with you, old dog. But with Cha-Cha, and all that washing, I finally had to go French and get a bidet.' She said she managed about one orgasm a week out of all those sprints, so I figured mankind owed her something, and I was the closest one.

'Are you counting, luv?' I said, one time. (*Only Yanks are allowed to call English ladies 'luv'. Any native gent would consider it working-class, and therefore unthinkable. Pity, calling each other luv is one of the many lovely things I love about the English.*)

'Well, don't stop, Jay-Jay, I'd love one more nice celebration,' she said, just beneath me. 'Keep your motor running. Do you mind if I get out my knitting?'

And one time she actually did.

'I hope you're hungry. I've usually been having just a pot of strong Assam tea and porridge, but today I had Suzie do a bang-up English breakfast for you. It's been a long time, hasn't it? You still swimming?'

'Not for a week. You?'

'Not for months.'

Swimming was the only other sport Annie and I had in common, along with a great affection. We had met in the Club pool, and mainly because she had a little boy with her. That in itself was typical, because she was taking care of him for somebody. I ended up trying to fix his backstroke, and one thing led to another. A wet swimsuit, or 'bathing costume' as the English used to say, brought out the full glory of Annie's firm, ample bosoms. Very sensitive, too, as I discovered, and capable of absorbing huge pleasure.

We walked in through the kitchen, in the old part of the house, hundreds of years old, and it must have been built for midgets. I remembered to duck for the doorways, to spare my perpetually bruised forehead. Suzie, a bright, blonde, muscular country girl, in jeans and green wellies (*rubber boots to you*) was standing by the

Aga, one of those incredible English coal stoves. Don't laugh, Gwenny and I had one in St George's Hill. Half-a-dozen different compartments, with different temperatures. Fantastic for cooking.

Suzie was surrounded by pans and dishes, but she glanced away for a second when I said hello. 'Hello, Sir, nice to see you again.'

We sat at a fine old oak refectory table and looked out at the shining meadow through a leaded glass window.

Suzie started bringing in the kippers and kidneys and streaky bacon (*which is the only kind of bacon you Yanks know*), and gammon (*the kind you usually don't*), and grilled tomatoes, and fried potatoes, and Eggs Benedict.

'That's English?' I said.

'That's Suzie. She's taking a course from the Council in *cordon bleu*.'

'That's *Europa*.' Later I said to Suzie, 'The eggs were *formidable*, Suzie.'

'*Merci, M'sieu*,' said Suzie rather closer to mercy than *merci*.

'What's this about burglars?' I asked Annie.

'I don't think there's much to it.'

'Jamie was excited. She has a theory somebody is trying to rape the Lordleigh maidens.'

'She sent you here for that, Jay-Jay? You want to go upstairs after breakfast?'

'Just for a sprint,' I said. We both knew we were kidding and hadn't the slightest intention. I have never had that kind of insulting sex with a woman, and never will, and Annie knew it. If I'd pressed the point, she'd have gone along with a warm, friendly two-way job, for old times' sake, and it would have been affectionate, and lovely, with celebrations for everybody.

'Actually, nothing was taken. You want to see?'

She took me back to an old cloakroom, where there were things like shooting sticks and Wellington boots and croquet mallets. I don't think Annie every threw anything away.

'Whoever it was, was rummaging around in here, and I suppose this was what he was looking for.'

It was what the English call a 'strong-box', a black rectangular steel container with rounded corners, big enough to hold a stack of documents about four inches high. Many years before, I had asked my bank in Weybridge for a safe deposit box, and they said they didn't have any, but if I brought them a strong-box they would keep it for me, for nothing, in their strongroom.

'You still use this old thing?' I asked.

'I should have taken it back to the bank. And now I'm going to have to buy a new one.'

I could see it had been broken open, probably with something like a crowbar. They're not really very strong.

'You should find a proper safe deposit box. My bank has got them now.'

'But look,' she said, taking off the broken lid. 'As far as I can remember, nothing is missing.'

I could see documents and legal papers, and pieces of jewellery, the usual stuff.

'What's the most valuable thing?'

'Probably the debentures, from the Club. The City papers, the shares and bonds and all that are with my broker, who is now in Knightsbridge. It wouldn't be possible for him to sell the debentures on the Stock Exchange.'

'So, strictly speaking, they're not worth anything to a burglar.'

'Well, he couldn't sell them.'

'Does it look as though these things have been shifted around?'

'Those are the debentures on the top, and I know they weren't on top before.'

'Why would he be interested in them, if he couldn't sell them?'

'Well, sell them or no, they are becoming pretty valuable now. When I saw them sitting up there, yesterday, Jay-Jay, I read the small print for the first time. Whoever wrote those debentures knew how to do a really strict *dressage* on small print, and make it dance. And at the time the Club must have needed the money so much they could get away with it. You might be somewhat surprised to know how much of the Club I own, and Heaven only knows how much the Club is now worth. It could be fifty times as much as when these debentures were written.'

'Paper profits for you, Annie.'

'Perhaps. But why would anybody go to all that trouble to look at these?'

'To see exactly how many shares you've got. Jamie said the burglar was driving an Aston.'

'A boy said he saw one in the bushes. Couldn't have been there long.'

I told Annie about the other crazy stories.

'Well,' she said, 'I'll bet they all have one thing in common. All those maidens at risk are probably big holders of debentures. The debenture-holders, together, own the Lordleigh Club.'

'And who owns the most?'

'Oh, I don't think there's any doubt. Letisha, Lady Mountvale to you. I believe it's said that you were rather close to Tish at one time.'

'Very. We were doubles partners for a while.'

'I wasn't thinking so much about tennis.'

'Believe me, Annie, tennis with Tish keeps your plate full. Bossiest doubles partner I ever had. But great. She was always right, she never missed more than one shot a fortnight and ran like a jack rabbit. We always won, in spite of me.'

'A couple of silver cups, yes? And that was all, just the tennis?'

'Squash, too, in the winter.'

'All right, old dog.' She kicked me, gently, with her boot, being careful with the spur, which just touched my leg, and lingered, still spurring for about two seconds, without hurting. A *dressage* spur is not very sharp. Annie knew me *very* well. 'You want me to *make* you talk?' Low chuckle. Smile. 'I'm going to run over to Molly Kerry's. Remember? She used to do my ironing.'

'I think.' Annie had a whole list of people who counted on her for everything. I couldn't begin to keep them all straight.

'Bad leg. I promised to bring her an elbow cane. I've got the top down on the Morgan. Lovely day. Join me?'

'Wish I could, Annie. I always feel good with you. I've got business with Max. I may even have to have some with Tish, now.'

'Give Maxie my love. Listen to me, Jay-Jay, you keep away from Tish. I like you too much. She can own people. She *does* own people.'

'Anybody owned by Tish wants to be.'

'Explain that.'

'You're too young, luv. Tish is an amazing woman. When she was president of the Club she made some big changes. Only Tish could have got us the indoor pool, or the tennis clinic for kids, or this whole new deal for young marrieds.'

'So why did they throw her out?'

'It was a close vote. Even the people who don't like her admit she did a good job.'

'Nobody likes to be walked over.'

'You'd be surprised.'

'Now what in Heaven's name does that mean, Jay-Jay?'

'Heaven has nothing to do with it. I love you, Annie. Will you be my mother?'

'You certainly need one, old dog. I'll bet you've got a lot of ice to break, somewhere.' She sighed. 'Come to breakfast, any time. Tomorrow it's porridge, and yoghurt, and if you can behave yourself, eggs *benedict*, just for Suzie.'

# Six

What I didn't want to tell anyone yet was that I already had the invitation from Tish to one of her big Do's. I was abnormally curious, since it was the first one I had had for some time. Since *the* time, the great Tish time you might say. It was the standard, engraved invitation, no comment, nothing written on it by hand, just the printed RSVP. Needless to say, I certainly didn't suspect it had been organized for my benefit. They weren't, even in those days *when*. And in those days, invitations? More likely, a ten-second ring. 'Eight, Jo-Jo. And don't be late, darling.'

I controlled myself. Perhaps a new social secretary had just found my name on an old list, and nobody had said, 'Oh, for God's sake, no more, not any longer!' Maybe the new girl hadn't heard how I had been flogged out of the palace, in a manner of speaking.

Well, the only way to play it was dead-pan, a formal reply, in the third person, would be pleased to accept Lady Mountvale's kind invitation, and so on, and see if her minions would toss me into the moat, so to speak. It was a chance I had to take, and overwhelmingly worth the risk.

The temptation was irresistible, even forgetting Tish herself, which was impossible, and of course it would certainly not be a *tête-à-tête*. There were usually more than a dozen around the great table. There might even be a stray Royal, if one were handy, and hungry for the best food in the Home Counties. But there were interesting people, too, maybe a wandering Nobel, a worried Minister, the latest playwright who wasn't bare-footed, or a *prima ballerina* who could read and write.

And Tishia, Tishia, I didn't dare bring her to mind. What if she really did want me back? Did I want to go back, after all that had happened? And for what? She could have phoned me, but that was not the way Tish would have done it. It would have to be special. An order, engraved. Be here.

Tish was the only woman I knew who was as beautiful as Gwenny, but they were as different as two beautiful women could be. Gwenny had been soft and affectionate. Tish was sharper, and a bit harder, but hard-bright-elegant, the way a diamond is, and of course hungrier than Gwenny, who had love but no hunger at all. Tish could be voracious. Just thinking about Tish made my pulse beat faster.

Once it was always tails and white tie at Tish's, but the invitation said *black tie*. Tuxedo is an American word, requiring subtitles. Madeleine saw me on the way out. 'Oh, I say, Joseph, you should dress for dinner more often. You're quite stunning.'

I kissed her. 'Nowadays it has to be something special, Madeleine. I'm going to Tish's.'

She stepped back, very surprised and trying to hide it. 'Really? Really, Joseph?'

'Really.'

'Oh, I'm so glad. You're back again? In what capacity, Joseph?' Eyebrows raised, lovely impish smile.

'Hmmmmm?' Look of mild outrage. Tongue slightly in cheek.

'Forgive me, my dear. Do give her my love. I'm sure you'll give her yours. Oh, yes, that *is* something special. I'll bet the tabloids would like to know. Maybe they do already. Will they put TISH AND JO-JO on the front page again? You'll tell me all about it.'

'Yes, I promise. There should be some interesting people. There always are – ' I stopped. 'Well, there always *were*.'

Of course Madeleine had known about Tish and me. Everyone in the Club knew about our tennis, and of course everybody had read what the papers said about us. Madeleine, naturally, knew even more.

Mountvale Park was less than twenty minutes away, in the direction of Windsor. I knew the way. I had that wonderful feeling of anticipation that I always had when I knew I would be seeing Tish. There was nobody quite like her. I had to remember she was actually half-American, although she was born here. She had even been born into a sort of half-title; she had started as an 'honourable' because her father was a threadbare Earl who had been bought by her American mother. Some say it's being done now with Visa cards.

There was no question the two lovers needed each other deeply. Tish's mother, Clarissa, had told herself she needed deeply to be a Countess; no one in Kansas had ever been one before. His need was just as great. If he didn't do something about the roof, the whole place would fall in, and Clarissa was the only way he could think of to raise the money. He certainly knew of no way to make any himself and she seemed to have as much of it as he could imagine.

Actually Clarissa didn't have any *real* money, less than

a million, or hardly enough today to lease, for less than forty years, a tired old four-bedroom flat in Belgravia, without even a place to put the car. But it seemed a fortune to him at the time, he couldn't even see to the far side of it. And he didn't look so bad to her, either, considering. He had an Earlish look, the way she expected an Earl *should* look. You could tell by the lovely vague stare, the bristly moustache, and the scent of down-market *panache*. She had had her heart set on a Duke, but they were all definitely beyond her price range. So, all right. It was a bargain Countess-ness, the best she could afford.

You could hear the long-horn beetles, the scourge of the stately homes, chewing on the roof timbers. Clarissa's first act as Countess, after the honeymoon (to Harrogate) was to bring in the man from Rentokil, who gave the whole place his most expensive spraying, and handed the Earl a certificate, which looked like a US college diploma, and was in fact a twenty-year guarantee. His certificate on Clarissa was less suitable for framing.

The money lasted while the Honourable Letisha went to Roedean, regarded as the fanciest school for young ladies, down near Brighton, wearing a rather ugly uniform, then to Switzerland to Aiglon, near Villars, to be 'finished' in French, and finally to Cambridge, where she surprised everyone by winning a First. I had all this from Tish, in the days *when*. She loved the fragile Earl, and pitied him, too, for being married to her mother, whose speech she always found more strident than that of anyone she knew.

By this time the money, in collapsing American dollars, was running very thin, and Clarissa realized that their principal asset was Letisha, who had become so absolutely ravishing that she could easily have become Miss Universe, or Miss Galaxy, if Honourables went in for that sort of thing.

You realize that this is a deliberate ploy to keep you in suspense, when you want to go straight to Tish, but it is also necessary. It might be dangerous, or at least frightening just to bump into her without any warning, or rational explanation of the incredible way she got where she did, to a position so close to being a Royal that there wasn't much in it. Rather better off than some of them. What you have to understand is the Wally Simpson Syndrome, and Tish's mother, Clarissa, did understand it all too well.

Clarissa was no fool, even if she often sounded like one. In her American university she had studied psychology, both normal and abnormal. She brought this knowledge to England, where she was delighted to discover that practically no one knew what she was talking about. This left the whole field surprisingly empty, and Lord Mountvale, incredibly, a sitting duck. I've done both the normal and abnormal, too, with Professor Bunch, in St Louis, and found, as Clarissa did, that as far as the English were concerned, I might as well have been talking Swahili.

The English are not properly educated. I know; my boy has been through it. Up to just a short time ago, children were forced to choose, at an age when no one can decide anything, between science and art, and thereafter were forced to renounce the other one completely. It has long been possible for a student to spend three years at Oxbridge reading nothing written since 1492, and to graduate with honors, which is spelled 'honours' – and then feel qualified to run a company making carburettors, owned by his father. He did this by hiring an underling, called an 'engineer' in lower case letters, who had been to a polytechnic, and was therefore considered 'good with his hands' but not a person one would ask to dinner. This fellow actually understood what a carburettor was. In America you *would* ask the engineer, for instance from MIT or Cal Tech, to dinner. He might even be your boss, or someone you hoped would ask *you* to dinner.

In England you might ask the psychologist to dinner, but no one would understand what he said. The problem with psychology was that no one could decide whether it was science or art, and that left it between two stools.

Ambitious English mothers, faced with throwing their daughters on to the market, studied Burke's *Peerage*, the hitch-hiker's guide to the Lords and Ladies. Clarissa knew Burke backward and forward, but also Krafft-Ebing, whose *Psychopathia Sexualis* has items that Burke does not. If there is a copy of it in England, it must be the one that Clarissa brought.

Clarissa decided to look into the Wally Syndrome. The English wondered how a relatively plain-looking divorcée from Baltimore with no special brainpower could walk off so easily with their king. Clarissa shrugged: 'Of course. It's so obvious.'

Many people reported stories, some of them probably true, about the times when Wallis would haul off and slap the Prince she called 'David', in the face, or on the hand (when reaching bare-handed for lettuce, something *no* American would *ever* do) or on various other places. The Prince of Wales, accustomed only to deferential, curtseying members of his harem of married ladies, most of them far prettier and, to the casual observer, apparently much sexier than Mrs Simpson, was delighted. Nobody else slapped him about like that, and wasn't it nice? He kissed the swatting palm, and married her, in spite of his mother and Mr Baldwin.

Apparently he could not face the throne without her. True? Really, the slapping did it? Or was it simply her attitude of domination? *Something* worked, and the ladies who lost out were much lovelier. Dr K-E is full of stories like that and Clarissa was reading them, and showing them to Tish. (*I must warn you, especially English readers, that some of this will soon become unsuitable for the young, at least the English young. It should be required reading for various old ladies who are self-appointed guardians against sex in England.*)

You are now on the way to understanding how Tish could win the most eligible bachelor in Britain, the Great Tombola, British for Grab Bag: greater, many believe, than the prize won by that other American, from Baltimore. At least Tish made it stick, and didn't have to leave the country.

The prize, as everyone knew, was Lord Mountvale, who combined the many millions of his mother's property empire with his father's title, and various heraldic bric-à-brac, and fabulous Mountvale Park, considered by many to be the finest achievement of Capability Brown, a famous English country-palace magician. (The name Mountvale derives from some German family named Vallberg, as Tish once tried to explain to me. To Germans, a berg is a mountain.)

The main difference was that Lord Mountvale was no Prince of Wales. He could have attracted women by the chittering flock without even owning a barrow in an open market. He was handsome, with the body of a rugger forward (read, US: *line-backer*) and though he had no more intellect than the average Royal, he could read and write almost as well as anyone.

Naturally mothers were throwing débutante daughters at him by the bunch, and several of them were almost sticking. No one thought that Letisha, the pretty daughter of a forgettable Earl, had a chance.

Clarissa and her daughter Letisha moved in the tackier outer circles of this group, and they rubbed elbows occasionally with Wimpole, Lord Mountvale, who was even a member of Lordleigh, as his father had been, though Letisha had never met him there. He spent very little time near the tennis courts, a bit more down by the paddock, and most of it away at Windsor, playing polo. His few personal friends at the Club called him Pokey. Tish had met him only at catch-alls like garden parties and royal marriages. She was not overwhelmed, but he was certainly a beautiful piece of man, and she did like him, fortune and Mountvale or no. Certainly a tempting target.

Clarissa, famous for her intuition, had a hunch. First she just said 'Hmmmmm!' to herself, after observing Mountvale carefully. And later she muttered, 'Well, it *could* happen again.' Although she knew that was too good to be true.

'What could happen again, Mother?' Letisha asked.

'I'll try to explain it to you, dear. Hand me that book, will you please?'

'The Burke, Mother?'

'I was thinking more of Dr Krafft-Ebing, dear.'

(I am recreating this dialogue from words I found between the lines of things Tish said to me privately in the days *when*. Pillow talk.)

Tish had her mother's intuition, and then some. And she understood what Clarissa thought she should do. Her first reaction was – no. Wimpole seemed such a bountiful physical specimen, and such a nice man. She liked him very much, even without Mountvale Park, and all those garters and millions. It was not really fair to *take* him that way. She would try to do it *nicely*, or by using just plain, honest, simple, loving sex, and she almost did. But she was clearly being edged out by two or three really glamorous débutantes, with considerably better portfolios, coats of arms and real estate (*a term the British never use; the word is 'property'.*) One of them surely had him hogtied, and in the bag.

'I'm afraid, mother, it's now or never,' Tish said.

'Fire away,' said Clarissa, closing the book.

The first tentative slap echoed in the corridors of Mountvale House, and Letisha held her breath. Wimpole looked at her as he had never looked at her before. And then kissed her. After that, as she told me, it was roses all the way, and some of them were on his cheeks. 'More on the left one because I'm right-handed,' she said.

'Did you enjoy hurting him?' I asked her.

She looked at me wide-eyed, and shocked.

'Heavens, no! Who do you think I am? Messalina? *He* was the one who was having the fun! Think of my poor hands.' This checks with my own experience. Though there are certainly sadistic men, I've never met a woman who liked to hurt, and I believe all Messalinas are the wishful thinking of masochistic men.

Then she said, as a kind of afterthought, 'Of course the trick was to make him *think* I enjoyed it. Otherwise it made him feel selfish.'

'Ah, yes. The caring Messalina.'

'I have to admit I did enjoy the feeling of power. And getting what I wanted. Whatever it was.'

Obviously the games were wide-ranging. Various

strange sightings were reported privately. Once, before the marriage, for example, Tish and Mountvale were seen, out of the corners of someone's eyes, sitting together on a sofa. Not unusual, you would say, except that her feet were in his lap, and she was wearing stilettoes.

Everyone said that the merely Honourable Letisha was not a ranking suitable to become virtually the Duchess of one of the foremost families of England, and many of his relatives tried to persuade him just to keep her, or to have some sort of morganatic arrangement, but Wimpole said he could not live without her as his proper wife, as Lady Mountvale, and the mother of his children. And Mr Baldwin was no longer available.

Clarissa, who had been down this road before, knew a solicitor, and the solicitor knew a barrister, because lawyers here come in pairs, one wearing a curly white wig, and they both reported that no stone had been left unturned. Lord Mountvale was, as Clarissa said, properly hogtied, or to put it another way, smartly, and happily brought to heel. Her heels, to be precise.

Letisha did have a real affection for him, though she was never truly in love with him. He was thoroughly, deeply in love with her, if that's the right word. They had two very pretty daughters, and she was genuinely sorry, and shed real tears when Wimpole went flying off that Alp in his Bugatti.

# Seven

Some of that enterprising little story was whispering away in my head as the Porsche's headlights lit up the towering wrought-iron gates of Mountvale Park, with their shiny black paint and bright golden points. One of Tish's servants, in a beautiful, almost military uniform, touched his cap and opened the gate.

'Good to see you again, Sir.'

'Good to be back, Harris.'

There was a sign saying, 'To the Car-Park', pointing off to the right, but we paid no attention to it. It was for the public car-park, for the people who came on designated afternoons and paid their two pounds to see the famous Mountvale Gardens, some of the loveliest in the world, though we would have been too early for the legendary dahlias. At one time the visitors came inside, too, to see Mountvale House, and all the Turners, but that was only on very special days. Tish said she was tired of having them traipsing around, and rooms cordoned off. She said she'd leave that to the poor devils who needed the money, and had to put in lions and merry-go-rounds to get the business. The Duke of Bedford and his charming French wife, as well as the Marlboroughs, used to cry on her shoulder.

'The cars are parking off there, to the left, Sir, just

beside the *porte-cochère*.'

'Thank you, Harris.'

Sometimes, when I was the only one, I used to park right under the *porte-cochère*, which Tish called the *Porsche-cochère*. It was nice, on rainy evenings. No need even to wear a mac.

I parked among the Rollers and Daimlers and such, some of them with resident chauffeurs. Tish would always have someone come to look after them, and bring them in for food.

I went in by the car entrance, and through to the big dining-room, the one with the Venetian chandelier and some of the smaller Turners. Tish was there, greeting the people, her hair freshly and shiningly gold-plated for the occasion, and wearing a modest little dress, modest until you noticed it had about half a million tiny little beads sewn on it beautifully, probably the work of an entire Italian town for six months. She looked as lovely as ever. As I kissed her formally on both cheeks, I noticed there were tears, well, at least a slight, new moisture in her eyes.

'How good of you to come, Jo-Jo,' she said. There were people all around.

'Tishia, Tishia,' was all I could manage. May have been a bit moist myself.

She had a tiny piece of paper in her white kid gloves. She pressed it into my hand, and whispered, 'That's an order, Jo-Jo.' And then she winked and smiled, beautifully, and turned to the next person.

The paper read, 'Stay after they leave.'

So naturally I was somewhat preoccupied during the dinner, which was about par for one of Tish's Do's. She had had live lobsters flown in from Maine, three different delicious wines, and all the rest to match. She also had me firmly imprisoned between an ancient poetess with a slight moustache, and the fat wife of an Austrian conductor. She looked at me from her position far down the table, with a twinkle, as though to say, 'That should keep you out of trouble until I'm ready for you, boy!'

When they all started drifting out I faded away into the library, the main one with the acres of standard, musty sets of Dickens and Trollope and all the rest, behind glass. Tish kept her own favourites and all the latest new stuff in the little library in her private sitting-room, off the bedroom.

There were more of the great Turner splashes of colour on the walls, but Tish preferred people, and she'd bought a few small Holbein sketches, a Lautrec lithograph, and a new Hockney, all of them almost invisible in the dim light. In even the simplest Holbeins you could almost psychoanalyze the people.

I sat in one of the big, comfortable leather chairs, listening to the distant chattering of departing guests, like a birdhouse at feeding time. Then it stopped. I waited. I thought, she's certainly not going to want to keep on all those damned beads. Let her wait just a bit more.

What would happen if I let her wait even more than a bit more? What if I just walked out? No way, no way at all. The anticipation brought her back to me, more vividly than before. A feast of ecstatic sex is a joy forever. You can summon it back like an instant, moving hologram, in three dimensions, together with the erotic sensations that make up the fourth dimension, the best one. Do I need to remind you of that? So I can step into that glowing mode any time, and no one can stop me, not even she. An instant replay, Tishia? No reply, which always means yes. Always. A satyr's game of solitaire? No need to be ashamed or embarrassed. Nymphs of memory are obedient, invulnerable, tireless, discreet, immortal, and forever erotic. Fancy sex, you might say. Your fancy can take you anywhere.

Join me, on three of the dimensions. You can always add one more of your own.

Hard to tell exactly where the great Tish *affaire* began. I knew her, of course, at the Club while Wimpole was alive. She had been a member before they were married. After all, everybody who was anybody was a member, and she was the Honourable Letisha, the Countess' daughter, and one of the best players in the Club.

After the marriage, we saw more of Wimpole, and I, too, was calling him Pokey. He would be with Tish, rarely on the tennis courts, but often in the Club bar, or the various dining-rooms, but he still spent most of his time away at Windsor, playing polo. We had never, like Hurlingham, had polo at the Club. Theirs had been historic, resulting in the Hurlingham Rules of polo.

Tish and I played some mixed together after she became Lady Mountvale, and after she became the Club president. Being Lady Mountvale, and a celebrity, helped her to be elected. She couldn't help the celebrity part, nobody can. After the marriage her pictures were always in the papers, as Lady Mountvale in the 'quality' papers, like the *Times* and the *Telegraph*, but in the impudent tabloids, like the *Sun* and the *Mirror* she was Tish, even on the front pages sometimes. A picture of Tish, especially doing something embarrassing, like falling down, or showing too much leg or a peek-a-boo breast was worth thousands to an alert photographer with a foot-long telescopic lens. Of course he could make even more with one of Di or Fergy and still more with one of Anne, the great Anne, falling off a horse.

Tish was safe in the Club. We had an unwritten rule that applied to all the famous members, the big titles, the highest ministers in the government, the show-business stars, or the occasional Royals. Inside the Club we treated them the way the Scandinavians treat their Royalty, everywhere. These lucky Royals feel quite safe to go into the supermarkets, or simply stroll on a public sidewalk, aware that the people know who they are, but are pledged to preserve their privacy. Imagine that in London, where the Royals are virtual prisoners in their palaces.

Tish had her own all-weather outdoor hard court, and a new indoor synthetic grass one. One day, when we were partners in the main mixed tournament, and it was pouring, with long waits for the Club indoor courts, she invited me to come out to Mountvale to practise indoors. There seemed to be no harm in it. We had never had an affair before she became Pokey's wife, and after that, of course, it was too late for me, or for anyone else. She was always faithful to him. I had a rule about wives anyway. Puritanical? I would prefer to say pragmatic. The husbands were my friends, and with lovely widows and divorcées in abundance, why be unfriendly? Many of the ladies, having become accustomed to a male companion, were lonely and simply crying out for attention. It was in a sense a moral obligation.

I drove out there in the early afternoon. It was the first time I had been inside the great iron gates since

Gwenny and I had come out to see the gardens, years before. Tish met me at the door, wearing a pretty white tennis dress. She looked beautiful, as always.

'Actually, Jo-Jo, I had invited the Browns for a four, but they had to cancel, so we can have a good, hard knock and a set or two of singles, and then a swim and some tea. Pokey may join us later. Come, I want to show you the new building.'

I was wearing a blue blazer and tan slacks and carrying my tennis bag, with rackets and clothes. The new building for the indoor court was next to the stables, and was both adjoining and matching the older one, for the swimming-pool. They both had bricks down below and mostly glass above. 'It was a present from Pokey,' she said. 'Sort of a wedding present. Nice of him, since he hardly plays at all. I'm still trying to get him interested.'

I changed in the little room near the entrance, and we began playing. The surface was marvellous, a cross between a carpet and artificial grass and a bit faster than grass. I usually beat her in singles, but she was used to the surface, played well, and just managed to win.

All that went very much as I expected. The mistake was the swimming. I had never swum with her in the Club pool, and I wasn't ready for the way Tish looked in the tightly clinging one-piece lycra suit, in a gold colour to match her hair. It emphasized her lovely breasts and her trim bottom and her gorgeous legs and in fact made her look sexier, to me at least, than if she had been wearing nothing.

I couldn't keep up with her in the breaststroke, the English stroke. All children here are taught it first, just as most children in the States are taught the crawl. They're very good at it, and often win the Olympic breaststrokes, rarely the free-styles. We had a jokey race, and she shot ahead, then I shifted into crawl, my old free-style stroke, and swam rings around her. At the end she shouted, 'Not fair, Jo-Jo!' and we clung together, laughing, and not in a sexy way at all. Well, not at first.

I had been very fond of Tish for a long time, but at that moment I was sure I was in love with her. And from the way she was holding me, I guessed she must have been pretty close, herself.

We separated, almost nose to wet nose, and looked right into each other's eyes, and said, together: 'No!'

'You felt it, too, Tishia?'

'Yes, and we can't. We mustn't and we can't, Joey.' I think that was the first time she called me Joey, and not Jo-Jo.

'Right.' And I meant it. 'But it could be fantastic, Tishia.'

She looked away. 'I don't even want to think about it. Let's have a few good athletic laps, and get dressed.'

We had not even kissed. I don't think we dared.

We had tea up in their private apartment. Tish said that when you lived in a monument like that, you needed to come down to a more human scale. This had started when they were still having the public in, to look at the building and the pictures. The apartment was definitely off limits to the tourists. Tish had had the private one redecorated completely in Scandinavian modern, in beautiful teak and satiny stainless steel.

'I thought we needed something rather astringent, after all the weighty period stuff downstairs.'

Wimpole, Lord Mountvale, or Pokey, was expected, and arrived for tea. He was a bit taller than I was, and was wearing a blazer too, his with brass navy buttons. He had been at Dartmouth, the British equivalent of Annapolis, and had actually served for a while on a frigate.

'It's good to see you again, Joseph,' he said with a friendly smile. He had the easy charm of the English gentleman. 'Have you been giving Tishy a nice workout?'

'She's too good for me, Pokey. When you play with us, if you ever do, we'll put you on her side.'

'It's the only way,' he said. 'When we play together I play in the middle, and she plays both sides.'

'But he won't do it,' said Tish. 'I can't get him off a horse. You should have seen him out at Windsor a few Sundays ago. Charles was playing, and Pokey was magnificent.'

'It's like playing tennis with Tishy. She does all the work. I have several very intelligent ponies who know much more about polo than I do, and they do all the work. They follow the ball and all I have to do is hit it. And after they go to all that trouble, then I miss it.'

Pokey was actually a superb polo player, with a high handicap, and everyone knew it. And so, like almost all my English friends, he always belittled himself.

Tish said, 'You wouldn't run yourself down like that, would you, Joey?'

'Of course not. Americans brag. They have to, it's a big country. If they don't brag, nobody will know. Pokey doesn't have to brag. Everybody already knows he's the best polo player around.'

We went on like that, and it was obvious that Lord Mountvale was a very nice man, and also clear that he and Tish liked each other very much.

And it was also very clear to both Tish and me that we

should not meet again, just the two of us, at Mountvale, or anywhere else except on a tennis court, where we could operate very happily together.

# *Eight*

So the great Tish *affaire* had not properly begun, and I was forced to gather what blossoms I could. Those were the days when I was working hard with Max and the animation, spreading sugar plums and Chocky Bears and dental work all over the British Isles.

This went on for more than a year, and then we heard about Pokey and the accident in the Bugatti on the Alp. He had been killed instantly. Actually Tish had just been about to fly to Gstaad to meet him. They had been planning to have dinner that night at Oldens. I telephoned her and she sounded frightful. We had played a match together a week before and had planned to play again when she came back.

'Joey, if you don't mind, I think I'll just stay home for a while, and sort things out. You understand?'

'Yes, Tishia, I understand, and I'm so sorry about Pokey. Let me know when you feel better.'

That was the time that Max and I began to go in for Art. It's the advertising disease. You are trained in many of the disciplines of art, which you are using in the most catch-penny way. The minute you begin to make a buck, you begin to feel guilty. You ask yourself, 'Do I want to spend my life doing *this*?' You are sure you are becoming a prostitute, and the best ones say, 'Well, if I'm going to be a whore, I want to be a damned good one, but maybe I could dabble a bit in honest wedlock.'

With the Chocky Bear selling chocolate jelly-beans to every kid who could crawl up to the telly, other clients were coming to us. Money was being offered. We were taking it. We began to tell ourselves we were meant for Higher Things. We were looking at the fine animation work that Dick Williams was doing, things like *The Little Island*. And the Czechs were turning out some beautiful stuff. It didn't have to be merely Mickey Mouse, it could properly be art in motion, and the possibilities had scarcely been touched.

'OK, Max, what do we do the Art about today?' I said.

We were sitting around Max's animation studio, after everybody else had gone home. All the big drawing-boards and camera set-ups were deserted.

'Why don't we do God?'

'No way, Max,' I said. 'Any adman knows God is out of bounds.'

'So who's an adman? Now we're on our own time. We're Artists.'

'So maybe we're serious humorists? Doing God, as Shaw would say, and taking the greatest trouble about it, but bouncing about with the utmost levity? I doubt it. Humour can't touch God either.'

'Why the hell not? Mostly, the more intelligence a guy has, the better his sense of humour. If there is a God, then he has umpteen times more intelligence than anybody. So, a terrific sense of humour. I think he would find most religion on this earth downright hilarious, treating him as a kind of sacred cow, instead of as a damned sight better brain.'

Max is a New York Jew. When I first knew him he

lived in Great Neck, Long Island. He had had his Bar Mitzvah and all that, but he wasn't what he would call Orthodox. I was raised as an Episcopalian, the Stateside branch of the Church of England. I had medals for going to Sunday School at the Church of the Ascension in St Louis. I never missed a Sunday in ten years, because my mother wouldn't let me. I was confirmed. I took communion, the sacrament of the bread and wine.

'Don't touch God, Max, they'd murder you. Even if you found the Big Truth, and talked to God, the real Great Big God, certified, and wrote about it, they'd get you for blasphemy, a breach of the local rules. Don't make any pictures of God.'

'Michelangelo did. His is still selling. Nobody got him for blasphemy.'

'His god was a great big hunk of man with bulgy muscles.'

'Sure. Mike was gay.'

'We had a picture of God in our church. Well, a third of a God, Jesus.'

'That's the triumvirate, right?'

'We called it the Trinity. The third member is a ghost. The picture was a stained-glass window as big as a house. Gorgeous when the sun came through it on Sunday morning. Jesus was ascending, going straight up. My dad was my Sunday School teacher, appointed by my mother, who was head of the Ladies' Guild and practically ran the church. I asked him when we were looking at the window, "Wouldn't you think his dad, who made the world, would have told him it was round? Twelve hours later he'd be going in the opposite direction." Dad said he'd have told *me*. After Mom died, he stopped going to church.'

'That's the problem,' Max said. 'Practically all the

religions we've got now were put together by people who didn't know the world was round. They're belittling God. I want to do a God that's big enough to fit the picture. The picture is twelve billion light years wide, and still growing, and he has to be the head of it all. If so, he would have to have a brain like – well to him Einstein and Wittgenstein would be like babes in the wood. Can you imagine how either of these guys would react to a Song of Praise?'

'Heaven on my mom's plan was the top of the dome, less than one light second away. You could get there without oxygen.'

'Right. A real God has to be a trillion times bigger.'

'And small enough to fit on the TV?'

'Being cynical will get you nowhere, Joe. You're not an atheist, are you?'

'No, I'm a hopefulist. I hope there's a God. I'd much rather have a real God than no God. The best one-liner on that is old Tom Huxley's: it is just as impossible to prove there is no God as it is to prove there is one. I'm still looking, and hoping. I notice there are no pictures of God in a synagogue.'

'Not allowed. No pictures and no statues. Not of God or anyone else. That's one of the Ten Commandments. No graven images. The old Jews were not even allowed to say his name. We had a lot of arguments about that with the Romans. They wanted to bring in statues of their emperors, all of them gods, officially stamped. We said no, and a lot of people got hurt. There are no pictures of God in a mosque, either, just squiggles.'

'OK, I'm with you in principle, Max. We'll try to imagine what a God of a million galaxies would be like. Then you can draw a sample picture, and I can try to think of something funny but majestic for him to say.'

It was a nut we could never crack. But being part-time Artists we had to try. We also wandered around in other certified-artistic directions. Meanwhile the Chocky Bear kept us alive and eating.

# Nine

Tish went away, and finally she came back. Of course there was a stampede for her. She was beautiful, she was rich, she was single, and practically Royal. If the tabloids couldn't find out anything true to say about her, they made it up. Is Tish going to be a Princess of Monaco? Is she going to marry a fleet of Greek tankers and a billion dollars? Is Tish somehow going to be the First Lady of the United States? Or the Queen of the European Community? No charge for asking any question, and it sold papers. Actually she stayed inside Mountvale House, and the tabloids had Tish-watchers, with cameras like the Mount Palomar observatory. I decided not even to call her, and to wait.

Then the phone rang. 'Tennis, anyone?'

And I said, 'Anywhere you say, Ma'am.' There was always the possibility that the line could be tapped. The tabloids stopped at nothing.

'We have to be very careful, and very private. I don't think we can even play outdoors yet. They've got helicopters. Come here, and not in your fancy antique.'

'I'll think of something. Hang on.'

I knew the fellow who washed my windows at Madeleine's, nice guy who went around in a track suit and running shoes. He sometimes ran in the London marathon. He came in an old beat-up Escort, and he often kidded me about the Porsche.

'I like your car,' I said.

'I like yours better.'

'You want to trade? For a couple of days? It's got to do with a lady. You understand?' He had the idea I was some kind of womanizer.

'No, but I can imagine.' He laughed. 'OK, but I'd rather do it for two months.'

I bought a blond wig, put on a red track suit, and drove to Mountvale. It was a suped-up Escort, and in spite of its banged-up looks, was almost as fast as my antique Porsche. Or, as they say here, it was a hot hatchback. Turbo. GT. Yay.

Harris, the man at the gate, was told by Tish that one of her tennis friends, a blond chap, was coming in an old Escort. He opened the gate, and I drove right up to the door of the indoor court. It opened mysteriously before I even got there.

'You need any windows washed, lidy?'

'No, but you could wash my fice if you do it loverly.'

The voice, if not the accent, was familiar, but nobody was in sight, so I thought I'd go in.

A squeal. 'Oww, you look smashing, mite!'

I jumped the Atlantic. 'You ain't seen nothin' yet, doll.'

She went up-market. 'You cawn't play tennis like that! You have to be predominantly white.' So very public school plummy that a raw Yank would need subtitles.

She was predominantly white, as they say at Wimbledon, referring only to clothing, but she was as lovely as I had ever seen her, and she was also in my arms.

'Oh, Joey, Joey.'

'Tishia, Tishia.'

It was the first time I'd really kissed her. She let herself go, and so did I. Her mouth was exquisite, and her passion was almost violent. Before we had slithered completely out of control, she pulled away, and said, quietly, 'Anticipation.'

'I'm not sure I can.'

'I'm not either,' she said, 'but let's try.'

We were both convinced, then, that we would make love, and if you are that sure, then the most delicious pleasure is not to do it full power, not right away.

We kissed, affectionately, lovingly, but not quite passionately, and then pressed together tightly, just feeling each other's bodies all the way up and down. I pulled her dress down, partly, and she pulled it the rest of the way, and I kissed her breast, gently, using moist lips on her nipple, and scarcely any tongue at all, and no teeth even, very gently. Like a baby, almost.

'Oooooh, dear! Don't stop!'

'Madam *must* realize – '

'And don't talk, darling.'

You can only do one thing at a time. I did the other one, too. But in a pure, nursling kind of way. The nipples were responding pointedly. In fact, things were happening all over, to boys and girls alike.

Now I don't blame Tish. She had been through a lot, and had been living a totally convent-girl existence for a long time. She simply couldn't keep up the anticipation game. She exploded. She took my face in her hands, and pulled it up to hers, which completely interrupted the careful work I was doing, and kissed me, with what I can only describe as violence – and then said, 'Ooops!' and ran off around the corner, and came running back.

'And what was that about?'

'I had to make sure the door was bolted. We can't have just anyone wandering in to watch us play tennis.'

'Certainly – ' I began, trying to say 'Certainly not – ' but there were lips in the way, the nicest way, and after that it was difficult to know who was in charge, but it was all right because we both seemed to be going in the same direction. Basically, down.

And down, of course, was synthetic grass, faster, as we had proved before, than actual turf. But speed is not important for all games, and it was nice to know there would be no grass stains.

'Take that off, Joey.'

Hers were partly off already.

For conscientious students, and apprentices, a word of advice. One watchword is consideration, and another good one is sensitivity. Take care when entering a new room for the first time. You will want to be invited again. Be polite, be gentle, the time will come later for machismo. And above all, don't hurry. There are no prizes for the one who comes in first, just a lovely reward for a lingering photo-finish.

There is no guarantee that a good player of tennis will be a good player at love but, not surprisingly, I had found that the odds on this were favourable. As a rule, the better players are the better lovers. And also, the stretchers make better lovers than the spoilers. Do you follow me? A 'stretcher' in tennis is one who makes you stretch to play better by playing even better, and a 'spoiler' is one who beats you by spoiling your game with nasty spins, or forcing you to play only the shots that you play badly.

Tish was a stretcher, and she played the game of love better than anyone I had ever known before. We were perfectly matched, and she understood all the ways to improve my pleasure. She performed a sensuous undulating movement combined with a knowledgeable constriction and expansion, in the manner of a wickedly skilful milkmaid, doing erotically with her body what the milkmaid does with her hands, wavelike contractions and relaxations, or, if you will, a wanton peristalsis. Not romantic? The action of bowels? Who said sex was romantic? We're talking of ecstasy in the nether regions, of physiological sensuality in a voluptuous *now*. The poetry comes later, recalled in tranquillity, the essence of lovely perfume left in the cauldron after the boiling of the petals of the flowers. The life-force is not simply beautiful, it is overwhelming, perhaps the ploy of a keen celestial Intelligence to populate the planets. Or could it be simply the survival of the sexiest?

I would have thought, from life with Gwenny, that a very beautiful woman is not likely to be skilled at the physical techniques of really expert lovemaking, because she doesn't have to be. She tends to consider herself an immovable package of paradise. No further effort is necessary. And that, of course, is not so. But Gwenny did add the great ingredient of affection, and what does that do to the formula?

Tish was an exception to the rule. At the very first, she was actually *too* good, she almost squeezed my control away from me while I was striving to multiply her pleasure. Altogether it was fantastic, but I knew, and she knew, that next time it would be even better. It had to be a co-ordinated expertise. It takes two to make perfection, and it was incredible that, on the first try, we were so close.

Our weakness on this first time was that our momentum got out of hand. We were bolting down the *piste* faster than our edges could stop us. We could not possibly have made the pleasure greater, but with more practice and more knowledge of each other, we could have made it last longer. We didn't quite finish abreast. She was ahead by a lovely nipple.

'You know,' I said, 'I think we could learn to like each other.'

'Let's try,' she said, squeezing me.

I had that immense euphoria that always comes after such almost unbearable pleasure.

'Do you feel as good as I do, Tishia?'

'Better, Joey, better.'

There was no doubt then that I was in love with Tish. Or was I just in love with sex with Tish? There's a difference. We lay there, side by side, holding hands, in one of those moments that you never forget, and then we went together into her shower, a nice European one on a long hose, so that you can move the spray all around and down under. The down under, most valuable at a time like this, is lacking in an American shower. We had a lovely hot, soapy time, squeezing together and laughing.

'There is a theory,' she said, in a terribly serious voice, 'that sex is bad for tennis. A famous doctor, whose name I forget, said that all dedicated players should *abstain* completely – ' she made this puritanical remark while doing a rather dignified bump and grind in the soap suds in my immediate vicinity.

'Abstain?' I repeated, doing what I could to counter her questionable gyrations.

'For an entire week at least, before an important match. Our bodies, you know, build up a supply of adrenalin, which is converted into noradrenalin, and sex uses this up.' As she said 'up' she emphasized the word with an upward movement of the hips.

'On the other hand,' I said, 'a member of our Davis Cup team, whose name will die with me, said he always tried to have an *assignation* – '

'Really, an assignation?'

'Really. On the night before an important match. Said it steadied his nerves.' I pressed myself against her soap suds in a steadying manner.

'Oh, well, it's all right then. Shall we have another in the soap suds?'

'Never,' I said, fighting for time, 'certainly not before tea, and no tea before a set or two of tennis, just to prove my point, and a swim.'

'That's practically forever. So it's goodbye?'

'And not on the floor, like pigs, but in a proper bed.'

'Can you do it in a bed, as well?'

'And *much* more slowly.'

'I do agree, we were *tout à fait* headlong.'

So, it was wonderful. We did play tennis, with a slight lack of firm concentration, and then we went to the pool. Tish made sure that the bolt was on the door. We had our swimsuits on when we went into the water. And after a few minutes we took them off and swam together and held each other closely and kissed and tried a water embrace, at first friendly, just friendly, in the marvellous weightlessness of water, and letting our passions grow, gradually, trying a deep embrace, just feeling each other, with a few slow, undulating, aqueous movements. The way porpoises make love? There are things you can do *only* in the water. Some use the deep water, some the very shallow. We tried both, and they were both lovely. But we were just playing at it, coming to no conclusions.

'That's enough,' she said.

'Yes, we don't want to spoil it for later.'

While we were drying off, Tish went to a telephone on the wall, pressed a button and said, 'Nancy, please send the tea upstairs, right away. Thank you, dear.' And to me she said, 'Nancy is the butler. She runs the house. She used to be my maid before the marriage. I sacked the male butler. He was stealing. I have taught her how to run a very tight ship. Everything goes *snap*! And Nancy knows you are not really here at all. In fact, I'm not either. Officially I'm not at home.'

We walked through a passage to the main house, and into a little lift that went up to the private apartment, the pretty Scandinavian one.

'You can trust Nancy, absolutely. She's a very bright grammar school girl, and absolutely loyal to me, and only to me. I had to teach her to be as demanding with all the servants as I am, and also just as fair. Pokey liked to see me in absolute command, it was sexy to him, I think, to have them all jumping to a snap of my fingers, the maids with crisp curtseys, and the men hopping to attention, like his sailors. The obedience has to be absolute, and instant. But they're all well treated, well paid, and well fed. Nobody ever leaves. I've decided to keep on running a tight ship, even after Pokey. It works, and in a curious way, they like it. But right now no one will see you but Nancy.'

'Is Nancy married?'

'No, Joey, Nancy's gay. I've known that for some time. In fact, I think that she has been about half-way in love with me. It's something like the Pokey syndrome, but tilted her way. She likes to be dominated by me. And one day she did me.'

'Really?' I was shocked.

'She had been massaging me, as she had done many

times before, and beautifully. And then she couldn't resist it any longer. I think I'd dozed off, on the massage table, and when I woke up, there was a lovely sensation. Oral.'

'No!'

'Well, oral is sort of the middle ground between gay and hetero, isn't it? She was doing it beautifully, better than Pokey. I just pretended not to wake up, it was so lovely, until she finished, and I came. I put my hand on her head, down there. She was crying. She said, all right I did it, and I love you, and now you can sack me and send me away. I said I would do no such thing. I put my arm around her and wiped her eyes. 'Are you — too?' she said, and I said no, my dear, but I understand. And the upshot of it was that we hired her very close friend Meg, a pretty little cockney girl, and Meg has become one of our best maids, the hardest working of them all, and a lovely seamstress, who can mend anything, even fine upholstery. And ever since, Nancy has been happy, and totally loyal to me. And no more incidents.'

'Is Meg in love with you, too?'

'That will be enough of that, boy!' *Snap!*

I pretended to cringe.

'There is the bed, boy. You'll be sleeping in it, and so will I, and nobody else!'

I could see there was room in it for quite a group.

'Just snap your fingers, Milady.'

'Now you're teasing me.'

She stepped over to me, and squeezed herself tightly to my body, putting her arms around me.

I gave her a spank on the bottom, friendly, but hard enough to make her say, 'Oh!' But she moved in even closer.

'You need somebody with enough clout to tease you,

Princess. Shall I snap my fingers?'

'Yes, command me, Milord.' She kissed me. 'Snap me any time, darling. You'll have your own room as well. We'll call it your changing-room. And it just happens that I can get to you any time I want.'

She pushed a bookshelf, shaped like a door. It opened.

'Oh, a secret door!' I said.

'Well, it's a bookshelf on a hinge. I think one of the old Lords must have had it for a mistress or something. We had it done over in Scandinavian. Pokey always slept here, in this bed, with me, but this became his dressing-room.'

I could see it had lots of cupboards.

'You'll find some dressing-gowns and slippers, and extra tennis clothes. And if I want you – look at this.'

She showed me a pretty needlepoint 'pull' hanging from the ceiling in her bedroom, the kind of thing you pulled if you wanted a servant.

'Now, step into your room, and listen.'

She pulled it and I could hear a little bell do an authoritative, but soft, *ding-ding*!

'That means you're ordering me in, Milady?'

'Of course, and make sure that you come, smartly.'

I went over to her, put my arms around her and gave her another gentle spank.

'Yes, I know,' she said. 'Pokey had it put in. For him. And sometimes when I pulled it, he came in, uniformed like a footman. And then I had to give him severe discipline. I even have a little dogwhip, which he gave me. I never really hurt him, of course. Nothing was too menial for him to do, and I do mean *nothing*. And when the game was over, and we had had good sex, with outrageous, but delicious demands from me, and celebrations for us both, he would laugh about it, and so would I. He said that some men went to whores for this sort of silly business, but it was much nicer, and safer, to do it in a family way, at home. It was very sound, psychologically, and he became quite well adjusted, in his fashion. His drinking, which had been pretty heavy, went down almost to normal. We had a happy, if rather unusual, married life, and he was always charming. I did learn to love him.'

While Tish was still in my arms, Nancy knocked at the door. I started to move away from her.

'Don't go, Joey. She'll wait. She's very well trained.' She kissed me again, in a leisurely manner, and then finally called, 'Come in, Nancy.'

Nancy opened the door instantly, did a crisp little curtsey to Tish, and wheeled in the tea. The first thing I saw was the crusty black bottle that could only be Dom Perignon, on ice, not yet opened. There was a pot of tea, as well, and an army of canapés, little tea sandwiches, smoked salmon, and enough other things to make either a bang-up tea or a smorgasbord for a cocktail party for half-a-dozen people.

Nancy was not dressed like one of Tish's maids, in little cap and apron, but in a plain black uniform-suit, with a skirt, a white blouse and black pumps. The Mountvale crest in gold was on the jacket pocket. She was just about Tish's size, with closely cut dark red hair, a slightly upturned nose and bright blue eyes. She was a very intelligent and efficient-looking young woman.

'May I open the champagne, Milady?'

'Please do, Nancy.' Tish looked at a little saucer of brownish stuff. 'What's that?'

Nancy was opening the Perignon expertly. This is like opening a safe that has been buried in a bog for a decade. She did it in less than half a minute. 'Chutney, Ma'am, there are a few curried bits.'

'Quite right.'

'The dinner will arrive at eight unless you phone, Milady.'

'Well done, and thank you, Nancy.'

Nancy curtseyed, and left. As far as I could tell, she had never looked in my direction.

'Well, a champagne tea,' I said.

'The tea is optional, Joey.'

'Delightful. Pity we're not hungry.'

After all we had been through we were ravenous, and the food and the champagne were delicious. We never got to the tea.

While we were eating and drinking Tish turned on the video and there was the latest animation from one of the real *avant garde* Czech production teams. I had never seen it before. There was also an antique bit of wonderful old Karel Zeman's early satirical stuff about his Mr Prokouk. I had almost forgotten it.

'And how did you find that?'

'I called Max, and he gave me a number in Soho, and they gave me a number in Prague, and I called them, and had it sent. No problem. Fascinating, isn't it? Now I understand what you're trying to do. It's a whole new art form, isn't it? Mainly I just wanted to show you I can do anything at all for you, Joey.'

And then, finally, lazily, we stripped off and went together into the great bed. There was an obvious improvement over our first rather clumsy encounter. And I do prefer beds.

'You see?' she said. 'It gets better every time.'

'And I haven't begun to teach you anything.'

'Ha! We'll see who is teaching *whooom!*'

We went to sleep, happily.

When we woke up, Tish popped a cassette into the video. 'How about an opera?'

'Which one?'

'I thought *Don Giovanni* would be appropriate.'

'I hope I don't end up the same way.'

Lovely tunes, though. Nancy arrived just before the hellfire, which of course Gio, or Don Juan, richly deserved, not because he 'loved' many women, but because he didn't *like* them, and *their* pleasure was purely incidental.

Nancy knocked and rolled in the dinner. As I recall, there were Chincoteague oysters on the half shell, probably flown in, lobster *bisque*, a Caesar salad, breast of pheasant, a lovely white wine, I believe one of Lord Rothschild's, and all the trimmings.

We decided to turn off La Scala and concentrate on nourishment. Nice to know we could pick up Gio again later, before he could take another breath, and happily see him go to Hell.

'Well! Are you going to like it here, Joey?'

'Give me time to think about that, luv.'

'I thought we might drive in to the Tate tomorrow.'

'Surely you're kidding.' I could see a dozen tabloid photographers, and TV cameras, and a front page of the *Sun* with letters six inches high, saying TISH AND JO-JO, together with the sexiest picture of Tish they could find.

'There's a new exhibition.'

'You mean us?'

'Oh, no. Just wait.'

There was no hurry. It was Sunday morning. A beautiful breakfast rolled in. The *Sunday Times* and the

*Observer* slid through the slot in the door. We tried to kiss in a virginal way, but it was no good, we hadn't the character to sustain it, and we decided to hold things to a modest little mini-orgy.

I remember thinking, at the time, that this was too good to be true, and I feared that it was too good to last. And of course it was.

There was more in the papers about the new paintings at the Tate, and Tish was quite serious about wanting to drive in.

'I do it all the time. *They* all do. You sneak out, it's the only way.'

Tish had a short, dark red wig, the same colour as Nancy's, and I had the blond one. We dressed down-market sporting-casual, nice sweaters, clean jeans and tennis shoes. Tish tied a scarf around her head.

We went down the private lift, and out through the servants' entrance. A little black Volks GTI with slightly tinted windows was waiting just outside. Tish drove us out through the back of the garden, and out the gardeners' gate, and on to the public road. We had escaped.

'Actually,' Tish said, 'Nancy has a GTI just like this. Get it?'

'Yes, ma'am. I'm with you all the way.'

We visited the Tate and looked at the new exhibit, which, in those days, had so much abstract-nothing that I could have done it myself, and Max could have done it better. And no humans at all. Then we drove to Chelsea, and strolled along the Kings Road. The punks with Mohican haircuts were charging the tourists, some of them American, for photographing them. We parked up near Marble Arch and walked over to Speaker's Corner in Hyde Park to watch some of the loonies, and then drove over to the Fulham Road to a Pizza Express, where the pizzas are crisp, like New York Italian ones, and not like sponge-cake, as so many English ones are. We had two American Hots, with spicy Italian sausage.

'You see,' said Lady Mountvale, incognito, hoisting a gooey bit, followed by a drink of Peroni beer, 'it is possible to act like perfectly normal human beings.'

'Careful,' I whispered, 'your hair is slipping.'

Tish drove us back very quickly, in this little racing car that looked like something grandma would be driving.

'What's your hurry, luv?' I said. 'Anything on your mind?'

'Not a thing, Joey.'

'I keep seeing something that looks like a great big bed.'

'Must be a mirage. Who do you suppose is in it?'

The fact was that neither of us could wait, but we had to, and it proved, indeed, to be worth waiting for.

So the *affaire* was off to a blazing start. I stayed until Monday morning, and drove back home, to change into business clothes and go to Rambleys for a meeting after lunch, and a meeting-after-the-meeting with Max.

But for those glorious honeymoon weeks Tish and I were together as often as possible. She would come to the Club to play tennis, and would then sneak around the practice wall, and over to Madeleine's and up the back stairs to my flat. Of course Madeleine knew, and being Madeleine, kept absolutely mum, giving me a wink and a smile.

But there was something very *back stairs* about it all.

'You know, Tishia,' I said to her one day when we

were in bed, 'a big tycoon often used to have a dolly on the side whom he called a *mistress*, and she was in *addition* to his wife. What would you call a gentleman in a situation like that, a *mister?*'

Tish looked at me closely, across the pillow. 'Well, not unless the lady had a husband, Joey.'

'What if she got one?'

'Where would she find one?'

'A *suitable* one?' I said. 'I'm not sure one exists.' I knew very well she could never consent to being Mrs Jo-Jo. And who could blame her?

'It does worry Clarissa,' she said. 'There are very few eligible kings left.'

'You may have to settle for a prince.'

She patted me on the head. After all, I was her new toy, one of the nicest things she'd bought lately. 'I do love you, Joey.'

'And I love you, Tishia.'

'Well, then, don't stop, darling. Just keep on doing *that.*'

And that, I assumed, was an order, as to a footman. *Snap!*

I almost said, 'Yes, Milady.' But I didn't. I just kept on doing it. After all, what *she* was doing was wonderful, as well.

One day when we were in bed together, Tish said, 'You do like the Riviera, don't you?'

'Love it.' Gwenny and I had been there many times together.

'It's getting pretty nasty in England now. Why don't we go down?'

'To your place?' She had shown me some pictures of the gorgeous apartment she and Pokey had bought in

Cannes. She had overseen the décor herself. It must have been worth millions.

'Well, that might be a bit public, Joey. And you do prefer rock swimming, don't you?'

'Yes, I hate beaches.' I was beginning to get the picture.

'Cannes is all pools and beaches. Pretty dull for you.'

And somebody might see me with her.

'I was thinking more about the Esterel, Joey.'

'Yes, good. How about a long weekend?'

'I was considering a fortnight, or more. Beginning a week from Friday.'

'No way, Tishia. I'm a working man, and we have some important meetings at Rambleys then.'

'Maybe I could help you out on that, darling. I might have a word with Chubby.'

'Chubby?'

'Your Chairman, Joey. I'll bet I could even sit in his presence. He'd give anything to be invited to one of my Do's. I could twist his arm a little.'

'Dammit, dammit, Tishia, you can't do things like that!'

Tish rolled her eyes up in the direction of Heaven, and then said, in a lazy manner, 'Would you like to see me try, darling?'

I knew very well she could. She could even *buy* Rambleys, throw out the Chairman, put me in his office, and make him my office boy. And then I would truly be her own private poodle. *Snap!*

'No, I would not like to see you try.'

'Oh, you're angry.'

'Yes. And I cannot go to France with you a week from Friday.'

'Would you like me to take someone else instead?'

'Go ahead.' I turned my back to her.

There were several moments of chilled silence, followed by a sniffle and the voice of a spanked little girl. 'When *can* you go, Joey?'

So I had won that round, at least.

'I'll have to work it out.'

'I'll change the reservations.'

'You mean you've got them already?' Without even telling me?'

'Just the flight tickets, darling. Let me know your new dates.'

I did want to go. The best I could do was one full week and two long weekends, after our big meetings, so we settled on that. Tish and her minions made all the arrangements. We took her little GTI to the parking garage at Heathrow, and flew to Nice, wearing our down-market sport clothes. At Nice Tish had arranged for us to be met by another very fast hatchback, this time a suped-up Renault 5.

'I'll drive, Joey, I know the way.'

The driving in France is much faster than in England, where there is a seventy mile an hour limit. And with Tish it was even faster than that. She drove on to the autoroute to Cannes, and swung off it to the eastern part, near the casino. She would let me go to the apartment because she wanted to pick up her mask and flippers, and a few other items.

We parked right in front of the very posh compound, all palms and flowers. The condominium buildings formed a sumptuous circle around the free-form swimming-pool, which included a pretty island. We walked straight to her building. She opened the outside door with her key, and went to the elevator. At the fourth floor, she opened the elevator door with another key, and we stepped directly into the enormous living-room. Her apartment took up the entire floor. It was beautifully done in comfortable French modern. At the far end were huge glass doors leading out to the balcony. She opened these doors with another key, and we stepped out to cushioned wicker chaises and parasols. Down below we could see the pool, and a few hundred yards away was the bright blue water of the Med.

I leaned over the edge of the balcony. 'Fantastic!'

'We'd better go back in, Joey.' After all, somebody might see us out there. She had told me she and Pokey often came here in the winter, and she had spent some time here after his accident. Mama Clarissa came down from time to time. Tish wasn't sure whether she would keep it. Might it depend on her future husband, if Clarissa could find one fancy enough?

I helped her carry some things down to the car, and we were off. The Croisette, the great boulevard flanking the beach, was, as usual, a slow parade of cars, inching along between the tall palm trees. People in swimsuits, and almost everything else, were dodging between cars. We passed the old, classical Carlton, the hotel on one side, its private beach on the other.

Tish said, 'Pokey and I stayed there while we were organizing the flat.'

Further along the shore was the bandstand, and the marina, full of the finest yachts of Europe. Far ahead we could see the bright red rocks of the Esterel. We went around the Corniche, a whole series of turns, with high rocky slopes on one side and white water on the other.

Tish was telling me about *La Colombelle*, the secret little house that Pokey's father had built for a beautiful

French woman named Chantal. 'Isn't that a pretty name? It sounds like singing.' He had an apartment for her in Montparnasse, and sometimes in the winter they would meet here on the Esterel. 'They wanted to be alone, with no servants, so how would they eat? Well, just down the hill was a hotel that had a very good chef, and Pokey's father made an arrangement with them. The French understand things like this very well.'

I noted that she said things like *this* rather than things like *that*.

Around the next turn was the small, deep harbour of Agay. Gwenny and I had swum there before. It was simply made for scuba, or just plain snorkelling.

'And there's the hotel!' Tish said. We could see it up above, surrounded by greenery. The sign said, '*La Baumette*'.

'We spent a few days there, years ago,' I said. 'Lovely food and beautiful swimming.'

We turned in towards the hotel, then Tish veered off to a little lane, hardly more than two ruts.

'Hold tight, Joey, we're going straight up.'

And so we did, with umbrella pines on each side. She stopped at a gate, and I hopped out and opened it.

I could see the little house, newly painted in bright white, with a red tile roof.

'It was boarded up for a long time, but I had it all done over.'

The little sign said '*La Colombelle*'. There was a picture of a white dove on it.

'That's Picasso's dove of peace.'

Tish parked alongside, and gave me the key.

'May I carry you over the threshold, Milady?'

'Please do.'

I put her down on the splashy red cover of a huge

bed. The room was small, and delightfully done in a rustic *Provençal*. A framed photograph of a pretty woman was on the bedside table.

'That's Chantal. Pokey's father loved her very much.'

Freshly cut flowers were all over, in half-a-dozen vases. A bowl of fruit was on the dresser. Tish went to the kitchenette and opened the refrigerator. There were cold bottles of white wine, and a salad in aspic, and a bowl of olives, and some caviare and sausages and Brie and Camembert, everything to welcome us for a bedroom picnic.

There was a long *flute* of fresh French bread on the counter.

'You see, Joey, they did everything I told them to do, and more! They probably remember Pokey's father, who must have been very generous to them.'

We decided to put on our swimsuits and go right down to the water. Tish led me to a little rock by the water's edge. It was clear, and very deep.

'The Romans used this harbour a lot,' Tish said. 'We know because one of their ships sank, with many of the big pottery amphorae, with pointed bottoms, that they used for holding wine and olive oil. These sank too far down for the Romans to reach them, but scuba divers have brought up dozens of them.'

We put on our masks and flippers, and slid into the water. A school of silvery little fish was all around us, more curious than frightened. We flippered slowly over the shallow part, and then, like flying over a cliff without falling, went over the very deep, dark part. Back on the shallow ledge, less than twenty feet deep, I thought I could detect one of the baby octopuses, the kind we eat as *calamari*, like chewy little onion rings. Their camouflage is so perfect that they look exactly like brownish rocks, smaller than a football, the tentacles all tucked away, like the legs of a pussycat. You could sometimes swim within a yard of them, and be fooled. I did a surface dive, and touched the 'rock' – and sure enough it scooted away, like lightning.

I came up, and Tish was laughing. She had of course watched it all, in the crystal clear water.

'I didn't see him!' she said.

The water was lovely and warm. Tish had a snorkel, but I never liked to bother with them. I just snatched a breath when I needed it. Flippering along like that in clear water is like flying. The rock formations below you move about in towering 3-D. Take off the mask, of course, and it just becomes a blurred nothing because your eyeballs are round, and the glass is flat. The first time you put on a face mask, or even goggles, you enter a whole new world. You never forget that first day. And you may never go to a beach again, except when the waves are interesting.

We flew about over the pretty rocks for a long time. We swam over to the place where Baumette people could enter the water from a big stone ledge, with a ladder for climbing up. A few of them were splashing around. One had air bottles on his back, and an aqualung mouthpiece. Tish and I had both tried it, and gone way down, and stayed there, but we didn't like the pressure and all the machinery. This was better, just flying, like birds, and going down a bit if there was anything interesting to see. When the water is really clear, you don't need to bother with the bottles.

We climbed back and went into her little bathroom, to take a warm freshwater shower. Of course, one thing led to another, but we had enough character to finish it on the big bed, after we were nice and dry and glowing. It was one of the best we ever had. And after that we raided the ice box. The wine was beautiful, and so was everything else.

Later, Tish telephoned the hotel, asked what they had on the dinner menu. She told them what to bring. It took two of them to carry it all. There were covered dishes, and under them were those little yellow night-light candles that the French use to keep food hot. I don't remember all the items that first night, but the hotel had a good Michelin Guide rating, and every meal was excellent: *escargots*, and onion soup and *bouilla-baisse* and *coq au vin* and *scampi provençale* and *veal marsala*, and a dozen other delicious veal disguises. The food, in fact, was almost as good as what Tish had at home. Wines? Tish was specific as to vineyards and vintages, and all in French. We drank very well indeed.

The next few days were just plain paradise. In between superb swimming and loving and eating we explored. We walked around to the pretty town of St Raphael and climbed up the tall watch-tower of the Knights Templars, to see for miles. We drove west to St Tropez, where Tish, in order not to be conspicuous, unfurled her lovely breasts for all to see. There were no stampedes. In St Trop, beautiful breasts are as common as elbows, but much nicer. So why is it so naughty to show them anywhere else?

We drove back to Cannes one evening in our London masquerade costumes, to go to one of the open air concerts beside the sea. Debussy and Ravel, the early, lovely French steps toward modern. We bought some of the grilled almonds that everyone seemed to be selling.

We were talking about a drive to Monte Carlo on the day that Clarissa phoned.

I could tell that Tish was being somewhat guarded in

her replies. 'Yes, Mum … Really! He *is*? … Yes, I'll phone you later.' That sort of thing.

'That was Mother, darling.'

'Oh, is she well?'

'She didn't say. Do you think you can manage by yourself for a day or two, Joey? Mother's at the flat, and I'll have to pop over for a bit.'

'In Cannes?' She nodded. 'Could I ride in with you? I could cut loose in town.'

'But then you'd be without wheels, darling. I think you'd be happier here. Shall we have a swim first?' In other words, the matter is closed. Wait for me. *Snap!* And I couldn't help remembering those words: 'He *is*?'

But first she phoned a hairdresser at the Carlton whom she called 'Gaby', and made an appointment. No attempt at any subterfuge. She was Lady Mountvale. *Snap!* After our swim she put on a nice cocktail dress and high-heeled sandals, not the espadrilles. Then a quick kiss. 'Be good while I'm gone, darling!' (And be sure you're here when I get back, whenever that is.)

She was off in the Renault, down the hill, quickly. She had a bag with her. And she had told the hotel to send the food, in single servings, to the house. So I was provided for. As they say, it was comfortable house arrest. Joey in aspic, to keep him nice and fresh until I'm ready for him.

And there I was, marooned without wheels, and without My Lady. My face felt expertly slapped, though she had never slapped me, nor ever used her little dogwhip. But my face was stinging just the same. Is that the way a mistress feels? Just wait for me, my dear. Be here whenever I want you, or else. And I may pop in without warning, just to keep you on your toes, and dutifully at my heels.

The first thing I did was to call the hotel to cancel the take-in dinner. I would be going to the dining-room. The more I thought about that, the better my slapped face felt. Surely she would not be back this night. I thought once more about the words. 'Oh *is* he?' And no woman has *ever* had her hair done to go to see her mother.

Surely I was entitled to a small prowl, if only for practice. I hadn't prowled for ages. I recalled having seen several tempting ladies on the Baumette swimming rock. Just for conversation, at least, to avoid loneliness. Or to prevent her loneliness? More than that? Not likely. I'd almost forgotten the technique of picking up a nice lady, politely, without hurting her feelings. The Club had made me lazy. Seduction? Ridiculous. No one can seduce a woman who doesn't already want to be. But *selection*? That can be fascinating, just to select the perfect chocolate in the box, whether you want to eat it or not.

We rationalize everything, of course. I certainly did not want to hurt Tish. One might even consider this could be for her own good. Making her jealous might make her love me more, if indeed she really *loved* me at all. In any case it was a way of keeping me fit and bushy-tailed for My Lady, whether I actually *did* anything naughty or not.

We had not been dressing for dinner, our informal bedroom feasts. But for the bar and dining-room of Baumette I would take care. I hadn't brought much. Not a suit, of course. I had one nice navy blazer, dark cordovan-coloured polished moccasins and good tan cotton slacks. The best-dressed British gentlemen are more likely to wear tan than grey with navy blue. There was one clean white shirt and the plain old-gold coloured tie. When I was a raw American I used to wear various different rep ties, varieties of coloured stripes, set at a forty-five degree angle. In England, of course, you don't ever do that. These are heraldic badges, and Old School banners. 'If you are wearing my Old School Tie and are not a true-blue Old Carbunkian, then you are a cad, Sir, and damn your eyes!' Not that he will actually say this, he will lift his glass, smile charmingly, and say 'Cheers!' But he'll make you pay for it one day.

I studied myself in our full-length mirror, and was more pleased with myself than usual. I locked our door, strolled down the path used by our food-bearers, and walked to the bar. I hesitated momentarily before sitting down. There were several couples. Usually, with the English, the men will be together. They are always slightly frightened of women. With the French, as with the Americans, the men are more likely to be with the women. At the Baumette, there seemed to be some of each.

This should truly be the *assessment*, the basis for serious strategy. One is really seeking a near-lovely stray, not the splashy star, who will already be fully booked for the evening, and the night. Find the shy maiden behind the potted palm, perhaps wearing glasses which can be removed to reveal wide, deep blue eyes, perhaps not yet painted up. Shapely, of course, nice legs essential, but perhaps visually destroyed by clumpy shoes. A luscious bosom, but hiding at first, under wraps. One who will really be seeking your warmth, and charm, but will be far too shy to say so. She will blossom and glow happily under your caresses. So much for the dream.

You'll never find these wonders all together, at any one time, maybe never. But that's what you're looking for. And at this moment you will probably not even consider that at least one female in the room may be doing exactly the same thing as you are. Prowling. Women, of course prowl just as much as men, but nice women know it must be totally camouflaged. They know that Rudolf Valentino is not at hand, but who, among all these fat old slobs, is the least objectionable, and has no other female in tow? Is there anything warm-bodied, and viable in any way? Might it even be carnal? Well, skilled carnal, and not just a quick, bungled bang?

Our eyes met. She, being a nice lady, naturally looked away instantly, and I, being a nice man, looked away also, but being a man I looked back. She was certainly not the little violet behind the potted palm, but I had an idea, all the same, that the evening might not be entirely wasted.

I did keep on looking around, but there were no shy maidens in tennis shoes behind the greenery. I looked back at the lady of the glance. She was, in fact, wearing high heels, so I assumed she hadn't given up yet. She was sitting alone at the bar. Obviously a bit older than Tish, but still very operational. Full-bodied, rather Rubenesque, ample bosoms. Good legs. Hairdo not more than a few hours old, a sort of chestnut colour, probably assisted. Obviously rich, but not flaunting it. Probably American, but not a raw one.

She was, in fact, the only possibility in the room. There was an empty seat beside her. I sauntered up in a slightly roundabout way. When she looked at me, I presented her with my warmest, cuddliest smile.

'Sorry,' I said. 'I didn't recognize you with your clothes on. Lovely water, wasn't it?' I thought she could have been one of the ladies I'd seen on the Baumette rock, but the ploy was for her sake, pretending that we had obviously met, and this wasn't a pick-up, even if she knew it was and wanted it.

'Yes, and you do look different, too,' she said. The new hairdo indicated she probably hadn't been there on this afternoon. American, certainly. A sort of no-accent Californian?

'May I sit down?'

'Please do. I must have you mixed up. I thought you were the one with that very beautiful lady.' So she had seen us.

'I was. My (*two beat pause*) cousin.' She looked relieved. 'She's off to see her mother.'

'Your aunt?'

'Mmm.' Affirmative? Deliberately ambiguous. 'Blasted little baggage. And now she's off with the car, and I'm marooned.'

She already had a drink, and I ordered a gin and tonic. We each had another, during which time I learned that she had driven down from Lausanne, where she lived. Had expected to meet a friend of hers, also divorced, at the hotel. Had heard it wouldn't happen after all. It was obvious that she would have preferred a male, but none was available. I could tell. Part of it was her lips, full and potentially passionate. And the eyes, a pretty dark brown, with a lonely look. What a nice person she was. I felt a trifle sorry for her, and at the same time sexually attracted. This combination I knew could be dangerous, or at least potentially inflammable.

Her name was Sandy, for Alexandra. Once upon a time UCLA. Yes, of course she knew the Lordleigh Club, which she pronounced correctly, Lordluh, swallowing the second syllable. She had been there several times. She and her husband, who was English, had lived in Virginia Water, and they played golf at Wentworth, until he was forced to go to Switzerland as a tax exile. And after the divorce she had decided to stay. She had an apartment down at Ouchy, overlooking the lake. She was obviously one of us, one of the wandering up-market Americans. And I'm sure she felt the same about me. We have little wiggling antennae, like beetles, and they say 'Yes' or 'No'. In this case a double affirmative, you may take the next step forward. And the next step was perfectly possible, we knew that we just might, but not that we necessarily would. Already we liked each other, and that's the best beginning. She had a room at the hotel. I didn't quite explain about Chantal's place. I just said I had a cottage up the hill.

We had a nice dinner together, and our knowing we just could, if we wanted, made it more enjoyable, more intimate. Gave it a kind of titillation. I could feel her slipper under the table. We had a bottle of good white wine, and we were mellow, but with all the food, no more than that. There was a pleasant warm feeling all around.

'Well, I do have a car, and I invite you to go for a nice sunset ride.'

'Delightful,' I said.

We walked down to the parking. She had a beautiful Mercedes convertible, with Swiss plates, marked VD for Vaud. Being British oriented, I went for the wrong door. She would be driving, and on the left side, of course. We decided to open the top. She pressed a button, and put a silk scarf around her head. She turned to the left, which would take us to Cannes, and I almost said, 'Oh, couldn't we go to Trop?' which was the other way, but we were off, and there was no easy place to turn on the Corniche, so I let it pass.

What was left of the setting sun was behind us, and the orange light made the blue sea almost lavender.

'How lovely!' she said. 'This is my finest moment on the *Côte d'Azur*.'

My arm was around her shoulders, and I gave her a squeeze. 'Mine, too,' I said, which we know was a lie, but a nice, lavender lie, and only one other person knew the truth.

As we approached Cannes, I said, 'Getting a bit cool. Could we close the top?' Who knew *where* Tish might be? Her eyesight was excellent.

'Yes, of course.' She moved us over to the side and touched the button. And in our new privacy, I kissed her, just a friendly kiss. I think Americans are *used* to kissing in cars. It is almost unfriendly not to. She responded so eagerly that it bordered on the – well, *affectionate* side.

After a few delicious moments, she said, 'Is that what you call a bit cool?'

We laughed, and kissed again, even more so. Now there was no doubt in my mind that if I wanted to, we could. The sun was down now, and the lights were coming on.

She said, 'Why don't we go in and see the lights, and then go back?'

'Fine.'

We moved on, and soon were approaching the Cannes marina.

She said, 'I was wondering if we could see it from here. His yacht came in this morning. One of the ladies said it was very exciting in Cannes today. He's really here.'

'Who's here?'

'Oh, *he!* Prince whatsit, Prince Ahmed, or maybe it's

Sheikh Mohammed. His yacht is so big they couldn't put it in the marina, and it's anchored out in the *rade*. I was watching it on *Antenne Deux* this afternoon. He came in on his own tender, bigger than most yachts, which he keeps hanging aboard, like a lifeboat. He owns that oily island over by Borneo, and his income is supposed to be at least a million dollars a day.'

I remembered. 'Didn't he buy the Savoy Hotel, or the London Bridge, or something, just with pocket money?'

'Yes, and he's certainly the handsomest man in the world. Do you suppose he's out there on the yacht now?'

'Could be,' I said. And who might be with him? 'Pity it's so far away. You can't even tell who is aboard, if anybody is.'

'Too bad, isn't it?'

We decided to drive back, and we were both rather quiet, and thinking. Should we? We could. She was very, very nice, and it would probably be beautiful. And yet, the more I thought about Tish, the more I knew that I simply couldn't.

When we stopped, at the hotel parking, we kissed again, very warmly.

'It's been lovely,' I said. 'But I think I ought to tell you – she isn't exactly my cousin.'

She nodded. 'Nuff said, darling. Kiss me once more and I'll run along.'

We kissed again.

She said, 'I can't tell you what a pleasant time I've had. One of my very nicest evenings, ever, and I was afraid it would be such a lonesome one. I needed that, just then.'

'So did I.'

'And by the way, if your situation changes – the snow will be coming to us soon. From my place to Villars, or to Col des Mosses is about an hour. Verbier takes a bit longer, and Gstaad a bit longer than that.'

'I'll bet the *après ski* is – delightful.'

'Well, that can be whatever we make it, yes? I would love to have you.'

'I'd love to come,' I said. And I meant it.

She tore off a bit of sticky tape. 'It's all on there.'

I walked her up to the hotel. And then I climbed the hill.

It was a good thing I hadn't. Amazingly, before 1 a.m. I heard the little Renault roar up the hill and stop.

I opened the door. She pulled off the red wig, and ran into my arms.

'Oh, Joey, Joey, love me, Joey, love me right now!'

I supposed that was an order, and who was I to say no?

Afterwards Tish was laughing.

'Mother makes a god of money, you know. And she certainly got that part right. I think he could have used Mountvale just for his polo ponies. His palace has a thousand rooms! What does she think my name is – Jackie? Mum managed to get him all the way from his ocean liner to our little flat. I must say, he *is* beautiful, and he does know it. Even has a bit of charm, and he is probably *divine* in bed, that is, when it's your turn. Do you know he implied that I might aspire to being his Number One wife? I suppose I might be the favoured one at least once a week. I almost slapped him, but of course I only slap people who *like* to be slapped. But if I'd *snapped* him a bit more sharply, I think he'd have cried. We had helicopters flying around over our swimming-pool. I think they did get us on telly from our balcony.'

'How did you escape?'

'Mother was very good about that. After he beat his retreat, tail between his legs, and fully covered by the telly, Mother took the lift down to Pierre and her gold-plated Rolls, with the shades all drawn, and drove towards Nice. I was watching on *Antenne Deux*. It took a while for the helicopter and the motorcycles to find her. What a parade! Then, at the airport, we saw her leave the car, and wave to the nobody in it. She had told Pierre to drive on to Monaco, but by that time the telly must have felt they had been bamboozled.

'I just relaxed until after dark, put on my funny clothes, took the lift down to the garage – and presto! I was glad to find you had been such a good boy, Joey.'

So was I.

The next day the British tabloids came out with helicopter pictures taken of Tish and the visitor on her balcony, and headlines six inches high saying TISH and SHEEKY! The story, of course, was entirely a work of the imagination. Would Tish now become a billionairess Princess? Had she topped Jackie in the money sweepstakes? The only true statement was that the great yacht had sailed out of the harbour. No doubt with the flag at half-mast.

We did stop off in Monte Carlo in our funny clothes. We had a whirl at roulette and their version of Black Jack, and then drove back to the airport at Nice, and flew home.

The honeymoon (with a slight cloud over the moon) did resume, at Mountvale and Madeleine's on the same back stairs basis. The loving with Tish was as fabulous as ever, but since that first call from Clarissa at Chantal's place I knew that I would always be her *mister*, if not precisely her poodle. I have never heard of the exact definition of *poodle*, but it does seem to have a connotation of dogwhips, and walking to heel, and perhaps even an oral overtone. She would never, but never, consent to becoming Mrs Jo-Jo.

Oh, I did ask.

'Of course I would be happy to make you an honest woman, Tishia.'

All she said was, 'But how do I go about making you an honest man?'

I knew I would, again and again, become Joey-in-aspic, kept fresh for My Lady, when she returned from the Hunt. And even after she had the stuffed trophy on her wall, would I then be merely her Chantal? Go down to *Colombelle* and wait for me, boy. I may be able to spend a few nights with you while Princey's at the conference. I expect absolute celibacy from you, except in my bed. Or else. *Snap!* Never said out loud, but I knew, I knew.

# Ten

The call from Clarissa came sooner than I expected.

'Yes, Mum ... Oh, he *is*? ... And what in the world would I do in the White House?'

Of course he wasn't the President yet, but Hefty Havelock, of the Texas billionaire Havelocks, was the bookies' favourite. So far he was just a Senator, but the PR machine of the Hs was spending millions on him every month. Already a campaign biography and a video documentary were out, making him a combination of Sir Galahad, Abraham Lincoln and the Gipper.

The Old Man, Crusty Havelock, who made the billions, said he could elect a pregnant sow to Congress, and many people thought the sow would have done a better job than some of the Havelock boys he put in. Hefty was a step ahead, though. He'd been Ivy-ed up at Princeton, and he had total charisma, movie-star looks, and at least a modicum of brains. Women all over threw themselves at Hefty, and Hefty knew how to catch 'em. The trick of seducing pretty women was in the family. Old Crusty bragged that he'd laid five hundred gals, white, black and yellow, and a few who'd only recently been men.

So Hefty was the most eligible bachelor in the whole world. Some wags were saying that once Hefty got in, it

would be better than Camelot, it would be Havalot. Old
Crusty was so sure he could get Hefty elected he was
already trying to have the two-term law busted, so he
could get his kid into the White House for life, and
maybe have it moved to Texas.

All they needed was the fanciest woman in the world
to be his wife, even if she only lasted until after the
election. After Pokey died, Old Crusty thought that
Tish Mountvale would be perfect, except that she wasn't
American. Then somebody pointed out she was
*half*-American, and that made it negotiable. She wasn't
rich by Texan standards, just comfortable, but at least
they could be sure she wouldn't be doing it only for the
money.

Hefty was flying over in a wide-bodied jet, complete
with a jacuzzi and a bowling alley. Somebody said he'd
be bringing a portable minister along too, in case they'd
want to get married on the way back. No woman had
resisted Hefty yet, and he was so sure of Tish that the
winning point was on the scoreboard already.


Tish and I were out at Mountvale on a Saturday, having
our usual orgy of tennis, swimming, and loving, when
the word came through from Clarissa that HH 747 was
already flying toward Heathrow. Later they said Hefty
would pick up Tish by helicopter at Mountvale, and fly
her back to Houston to meet Daddy.

'But, Mother, I haven't even met *him* yet.'

Clarissa told her they'd get to know each other real
well on the way back. And they'd probably spend a week
or so over there. Since it was getting cool, even in Texas,
they might wander down to Acapulco. His daddy had a
purty nice place down there. He'd brought it back stone
by stone from Italy, statues and all. (Crusty's missus, Ma

Havelock, had diapers put on the men statues, where the parts were showin'. Whatever was goin' on inside, she wanted everbuddy to see it was nice and clean outside.)

'I could go as your chaperone,' I said.

'You are going to stay right at Madeleine's and wait for me, Joey, and I do mean *wait*.' *Snap*!

'Yes, Milady.'

And at that moment I was sure for the first time that I was really a poodle. I could almost feel the dogwhip on my curly hide.

I was back at Madeleine's, watching on the telly when Hefty landed his chopper among the husks of the famous dahlias in the gardens of Mountvale House. Close shot of Hefty kissing Lady Mountvale. She did a head-bob, like a boxer avoiding a left jab, so the first smack landed on her jawbone, but he grabbed her chin for the next one, and homed right in on her lips, hard, taking his time about it. She could wriggle, but she couldn't hide. I had to admit she came up smiling. Hefty must have been mega-sex, with a big added power factor, plus unlimited bucks. Then he practically carried her aboard, and we followed the chopper out of sight, over the horizon.

I had a very empty feeling. If I was a poodle, I was a lonesome one, with nobody to wag my tail to.

But suddenly, somehow, I began to hear the faint strains of a Lordleigh version of The *Marseillaise*, The Internationale and the Battle Hymn of the Republic. I could barely make out old Tom Paine mumbling about sunshine patriots and the times that tried men's souls. My flesh was tingling. I felt I was becoming a giant. Well, a medium-sized giant, slightly grey at the temples. Was I a man in poodle clothing?

So I went and did it. I'm sure I was aided, in some way, by whatever Almighty there was. 'Look at the snow reports. See what I've done for you, boy,' I could swear he said. I Picked up the *Times* and turned to the snow reports, the size of a want ad. I could see that the page was glowing, like a burning bush, just that tiny part, in its usual telephone-book print. It said there was powder high, and powder low in Switzerland. You can say it was too early. *I* said it was too early, but I looked up as high as I could, and said, 'Thank you, Sir.' No reply.

I remembered the little piece of Sandy's sticky tape that I had pasted into my diary. Her phone number was on it. I added 0104 for Switzerland, and dialled the whole thing.

'I just wanted to know if the ski lifts were working, Sandy.'

'Oh, darling, if they aren't, I'll go up with you on skins.' (That's how they used to climb up the *pistes*, before lifts, with pieces of fur on the bottoms of the skis.) 'When can you come?'

'Tomorrow?'

'I'll meet your plane at Geneva.'

At first I didn't see her. I was looking for the Merc. Then I spotted her getting out of a Range Rover, which can climb up the north side of an igloo.

Right away I gave her a big kiss. Then I said, 'Where's the Merc?'

'I got tired of having the Touring Club Suisse put sandbags in the trunk when there was snow. Rear-wheel drive only, you know. This one has drive even on the steering-wheel.'

Her skis were already on the rack, on top, and mine joined them.

Of course there was no snow here, at lake level. The autoroute to Lausanne goes right by the airport parking, so we turned on to it, and drove along the south side of the Lake, called the Lake of Geneva by the Genevese, and Lac Léman by everybody else. For miles the grapevines rose up, terrace by terrace, on our left. The *vendange* was over, the grapes were gone, the vine leaves had autumn colours, and the fragrant juices were lying in huge vats, slowly becoming the great white wines of Switzerland.

'My trouble is,' she said, 'that I watch too much French TV, so I know about your (*pause*) cousin.'

'Everybody does.'

'She *is* lovely.'

'Yes. At first I was just her doubles partner at the Club.'

'And now you're hurt.'

'Now I'm with you, Sandy.'

'You're still in love with her?'

'Now I'm with you, Sandy,' I repeated.

'I'm going to be terribly careful with you, Joey. You like to ski very much?'

'Yes.'

'So do I. At first maybe just skiing.'

'Maybe.' I squeezed her.

'Don't you *dare* kiss me now. We're doing 130.' She meant eighty-five mph. So I didn't kiss her, not then. But we were in Lausanne in about an hour, and I kissed her in the garage under her apartment building. She was very, very hungry for love. I don't think she had had any at all for a long time. Switzerland is like that. It's hard to get to know people well enough to sleep with them. But she was proud.

'You stop right there, Joey. I've got to nurse you

along gently. And while there's light we're going to sit quietly and watch the view, and absorb a few jars of booze. I'm not going to feed you yet, I know that Swissair gives you a nice meal on the way, I've done it often enough, but I've got something tasty for you after the booze, a little *fondue Borguignonne*, that's the beefy one.'

'Yes, I know. I like it better than the cheesy one.' Gwenny and I used to commute to French Switzerland at snow time.

I knew this was going to be a nice contrast to *snap*. And I could tell she was just *aching* to be properly loved, but didn't want to show it. We would be gentle, and go slowly. But we were sure, oh very sure, we would get there.

The view was one of the world's most beautiful, and her cosy balcony was part of it. We had privacy, too. We could see out, but nobody could really see in. The lake, with plenty of sails still showing, was just in front, and beyond that were the French Alps. The spikey *Dents de Midi* were sticking straight up, with Evian barely visible, down below, at lake level. Plenty of snow on the peaks, and enough far down to promise very good *pistes*.

'It's exciting. The beginning of the ski season – and you, Joey!'

She remembered the gin and tonic, that English favourite, and she had little cubes of Emmental and Gruyère and some roasted almonds, and we held hands and kissed gently. I knew how she wanted to play it, now. We had it all right there, and we could take our time.

The sun was going down. We put on big sweaters and watched the harbour lights go on nearby, and we could see the faint flicker coming from the French across the water.

We went back in, where it was nice and warm, and I kissed her standing up. We pressed each other tightly all the way down. But no more, not yet. She knew the game we were playing.

'Now you're going to work,' she said. We went back to her kitchen, walnut-panelled, and all the tools were German NEFF, in gleaming stainless. 'There's the meat. You know how to cut it?'

'Yes. It's beautiful.' It was a piece of Châteaubriand, a super-filet with everything except lean beef removed. While I was slicing it down to bits just the size to put on the end of a fork, she was lighting the alcohol flame un- der the *caquelon*, the little stainless fondue pot, and heating the sunflower oil in it. She had already done the little dip-sauces with horse radish, and onion, and curry, and –

'Garlic, Joey?'

'Yes, if you do, too.'

'Everything together, darling. And now open this, please.'

She brought a chilled bottle of *Épesses* out of the fridge. It was a new one to me.

'Remember those empty vines we saw when we were driving by? Some of those were from the vineyards of *Épesses*. Not much of it gets out of the country. The Swiss buy it all.'

I opened it, and did the wine waiter's trick of pouring a thimbleful into the glass and offering it to her. 'Madame!'

'I know it's good.' But she tasted it, and handed it back to me.

'Superb!'

We brought it all into her sitting-room. The furniture was all nice English. 'Harrods?' Gwenny had bought things there.

'Yes, and Peter Jones. Most of it we had in our house in Virginia Water.'

We drank the wine, and we took the long forks,

stainless, with teak handles, and speared pieces of raw filet and dipped them into the boiling oil, for just a few seconds, and then into the spicy sauces.

And then we moved over to the settee to have a Southern Comfort. We both knew we were very close to where we were going. And we knew there was no hurry. We began kissing, *really* kissing, and when I kissed her breast, I knew that was one department where she could outdo Tish. She didn't move. I don't think she even breathed.

'Now you've gone and done it, Joey. Come with me, laddie.'

She pulled me into the bedroom.

'And light those candles, please.'

She had a brass candelabra, holding three new white candles. Neither of us smoked, but I saw a fresh box of matches. I lit the candles.

'Now don't take off a stitch until you turn out the lights.'

'Of course not, it would be unseemly.' I turned them off. In ten seconds, the clothes were on the floor and we were in each other's arms. After a long, undulating squeeze we were in bed.

I wanted to be sure that Sandy, after so long alone, was really *ready* for me. I didn't want to hurt her a bit. So I kissed her breasts for a while first and moved very close to her, to give her time to be ready. And then I truly joined her, and I could feel she was indeed ready. Very gently at first. There is a great deal to say for a woman who has a bit more flesh on her bones. She was certainly not fat, but very well upholstered. A really *comfortable* woman to be with; like riding an erotic flying carpet, with a spongey underlayer, and a sophisticated driver.

I suppose the main difference between Tish and

Sandy was that Tish was voracious, hungry, ravishing. Sandy was solicitous and caring. Did that feel good, darling, or would you like it better this way? Let me know what you like. I'll be your slave girl, master. Make me do anything. Make me do *everything*. We took a long time, and she had many celebrations, and I but one; but a lovely one.

In the morning there was no hurry. She always had fresh croissants delivered to her door. We had them with bitter English marmalade and coffee.

'There's plenty of time, darling. We can get to the snow very quickly. Come back here to me, and we'll have a nice encore.' It wasn't an order, just a friendly suggestion, which would be unfriendly to refuse.

There was no candlelight, only sunshine filtering through the slats of the venetian blind. For me it's always better in the morning. The undulating carpet was flying delightfully. And I never heard a single *snap*!

We showered, put on our ski clothes, and went down to the car. We drove up to the autoroute, which took us through tunnels, and on to the end of the lake, where we went over the great flyover, looking down on lovely old Victorian Montreux, built to suit the English. The view to the right, with Lac Léman stretching back all the way to Geneva, and the French peaks lining its whole north side – well, it is simply unbelievable.

We decided to go first to Villars, where most of the *pistes* are short and easy, a good place to begin the season. We left the lake and started to climb. Almost immediately there was a dusting of snow on the ground, which quickly became deep powder. The road itself had been immaculately cleared. The Swiss don't even wait for the snow to stop falling. Every truck has a snap-on snow plough. We could see chalets all around us.

Up in Villars, everyone was clumping about in ski boots and carrying skis. There were many apartment-house chalets, with balconies and pointed roofs. Sandy found a parking place. We put on our boots, and with the skis over our shoulders we walked to the cog railway. We dumped our skis and poles into the open carriage in front.

Ever since Gwenny and I first came up the cog railway, years ago, I've had that feeling of anticipation mixed with fear. You never get entirely over the fear part. You know you'll be standing there at the top of the hill, and it seems to go straight down. At first Gwenny was so frightened she said she wanted to cry. Of course we had started on the nursery slopes, with the pros, leaning how to snow-plough, and then how to do a parallel turn, and how to traverse a slope, to go across it and not straight down, and most important of all, how to stop, anywhere, any time. And then, for a while, you become too brave, and you break a leg.

We left the train, and there it was, the top of a hill, going straight down. The rat-tracks, the big caterpillar-type tractors, had flattened the deep powder. The snow looked very skiable.

'Follow me, Joey,' Sandy called, and took off, doing a lovely turn. She was much better than I was. For several winters she had been skiing all the time.

I pushed off, and after my first turn I felt better, it was coming back.

And so it went. We queued up for T-bars and chair lifts, and I was having fun. Once while we were waiting for a lift somebody called, 'Good afternoon, Joseph!' It was the Browns, two of my tennis friends from the Club. I introduced Sandy to them, and we went up together.

Afterward, Sandy said, 'Won't that get back to your cousin?'

'Yes, bound to.' I knew it would happen. I had hundreds of friends at the Club and many of them came skiing.

'You know, I think you came here deliberately.' She squeezed my hand.

'I came here to see you, Sandy.'

We had some sausages and sauerkraut and beer up at the top. From there we could see for miles. Once I missed a turn, and hit the snow, and had it all over my face. Sandy helped me to put back all the pieces, and we went off together. She never fell once.

That evening we drove back in the sunset and we had a hot, soapy shower together. We were warm and glowing and tired, all at once, as you are when you have been skiing in the sunshine. We went to bed, under the covers, and fell asleep in each other's arms, and when we woke up we made love in a wonderful, lazy way.

And that's how it went for three days. The next day we drove to Verbier where the *pistes* were more interesting, and more difficult, and I fell down once.

On the last whole day we decided to get up early and drive all the way to Gstaad. First Sandy called Oldens, and reserved dinner for two, and found us a room at one of the hotels. Then we started out. On the map it doesn't look far away at all, but the difference is that you can only do a small part of it by the autoroute. You have to follow the lovely little roads along the valleys. It is a glorious drive, with huge snowy mountains on all sides. Gwenny and I had only been as far as Chateau d'Oex where you can see from the main road the great panorama of hundreds of chalets. But we had never gone as far as Gstaad.

Sandy said, 'Gstaad is to skiing what Trop is to swimming. The skiing may not be as good as Verbier, but the *après-ski* is better. People come here to be seen, and to see famous people. It's just over the edge of French Switzerland, but it's so international that Gstaad speaks everything, and maybe English most of all.'

We went first up the cable lift at Saanenmoser, to ski, and then came back to our hotel to shower and change clothes. While we were walking about the town, we met another couple from the Club, and I introduced Sandy. So there was no doubt that Tish would know. We walked to Oldens, one of the most famous restaurants in Swiss ski country. The food was fabulous.

And on the French telly in the hotel, which Sandy understood much better than I, we caught up with Tish and Hefty in Acapulco, at Crusty's movable palace. They were arm in arm, and looked very, very friendly.

'Shall I turn it off?' Sandy asked.

'No, no. It's all right, Sandy. It's over.'

'Are you sad about that, Joey?'

'I made it be over. Kiss me, Sandy.'

We both knew I would have to go back to London the next day, for a meeting at Rambleys, and another with Max.

Sandy drove me to Geneva. I left my skis with her, and promised to see her again. And that I did.

Well, that was the end of the great Tish *affaire*. She came back from her assignation with the Texas billions. The tabloids said it all: TISH SAYS NO TO HEFTY.

The world was stunned. How could any woman resist Hefty Havelock and a billion bucks? I knew what Hefty's brand of quick-bang sex with everybody in skirts would do to Tish, and I had bet she'd be back quickly. I would miss her. There was nobody like her, but I'd had enough of poodledom, and made no attempt to call her.

By and by my clothes came back from my changing

room at Mountvale, all beautifully laundered and ironed. I saw her from time to time at the Club, of course. We smiled. We were thrown together sometimes in tennis tournaments, and it was always a joy to play with Tish, or against her. I kissed her socially, on both cheeks, whenever it was the thing to do.

But we knew, we both knew.

And that was what I was thinking. My life with Tish was flashing before my eyes. Because it was dying?

I was sitting in the great library at Mountvale, after Tish's big Do, wondering why she wanted to see me in her bedroom after the others left. I had better go and see what she had in mind. I had certainly given her time to get out of those beads.

I strolled out and up the great stairway. Not a soul, except a crowd of Mountvale ancestors, all of them dead, and all of them looking right at me. They hadn't had time to do Pokey. Tish said she planned to have one painted, based on a few polaroids.

I went into the Scandinavian private apartment with its great, wonderful bed that we had enjoyed so much, and there was Tish, in a natural, soft, sheer cashmere dressing-gown, her hair sort of shaken loose, and looking all over soft and lovely. I noticed there was another bottle of Dom Perignon on ice, in case anybody wanted it.

'Don't open it for me, Tishia. I have to be driving home.'

'Don't let it give you any ideas, Jo-Jo. I'm sleeping alone tonight. One kiss, before I give you my instructions.' But it was said gently without *snap!*

'A peck or a production?'

'I didn't know you had any pecks. I only remember the productions.'

I put my arm around her, and carefully let one thigh go between hers and then pulled us strongly together so that we pressed tightly from her breasts all the way down to her thighs. The throbbing, animal sex of Tish flowed through me like high voltage. There wasn't a thing under the sheer cashmere.

'That's not fair,' she said.

'You feel so good.'

'Mmmmmm. Oh, Joey.'

I kissed her, good and proper, and you can't do that unless the other side is playing ball. 'Tishia, Tishia.'

'No, no,' she said, affirmatively, and I thought for a second we had gone past the point of no return. It takes many practice runs to reach that peak of total synchronized ecstasy, and we had done it together so many times. I mean even if both of us had decided no, definitely not this time, something could snap, when you had had that thing before, together, and you knew you could have it again, and it was the most excruciatingly marvellous thing you could ever do.

Tish broke the string, or whatever that was between us. She stepped back and said crisply, almost like an order to a servant, 'That will be enough of that.'

'Yes, Milady.' But I pulled her back to me.

'No, Jo-Jo.'

We were even more tightly together and my thigh was firmly pressed between hers.

'One more kiss,' I said, 'and I give you my word, I will not go to bed with you tonight.'

I thought I could tell by the way she returned the kiss. Hers was so hungry I could just feel she hadn't been loved enough lately.

I pressed her backward, almost imperceptibly to touch the wall and moved my thigh even closer between her legs. I could feel her press forward to contain it. We kept on kissing, and I made an undulating movement with my thigh, throbbing and throbbing. I knew her very well, of course. I had been there before and I knew how all the furniture was arranged. I heard her moan, an almost helpless moan, but full of the quality of life, and I knew she was gone. I kept on kissing, and undulating, and then I felt it, that ecstatic shudder, almost an explosion, that I knew so well, from Tish and a long, long, 'Oooooohhh.' She had a huge capacity for pleasure. And then, 'Oh, damn you, Joey, damn you,' all very loving damns of course. I was still quite dry, and I hadn't even taken off the black tie.

'You, too?' she asked.

'No, darling, I promised you.'

'Is this the beginning of St Joseph? Of course I did say I wouldn't give you a thing.'

We sat down together on the settee. My arm was around her shoulder, in a friendly way.

'You just gave me a lovely dinner.'

'I don't mean that.'

'Oh, one of those. You owe me one.'

'You took advantage.'

'You want me to take it back?'

She sat up straight. She was Lady Mountvale again, about to snap her fingers.

'I have not forgiven you. I should throw you out. I should ring for Harris.'

Harris, down at the gate, was a black belt, or something like that. Nice guy, too. But he certainly would have come, on the double, and he would have done anything she ordered him to do. Like to me. 'Don't hurt him any more than you have to, Harris.'

'Don't bother Harris,' I said. 'I'll go quietly. Ma'am.'

'You *can't* go yet, Jo-Jo. Stay until I'm finished with you. And I haven't forgiven you. I'm not sure I'll ever forgive you. I will not share anybody with anybody else. You cannot be half mine.'

'I decided the same thing, Tishia. I'm not coming back.'

'I guessed that. Pity, isn't it?'

'Yes.' When a really great *affaire* ends, it's a dreadful waste of know-how. And, of course, an ending of joy.

'I'm changing the subject, Joey. You must be aware of the things that are happening.'

'You mean the rape of the Lordleigh maidens?'

'Tell me everything you know. Please.'

I told her all I've just told you, censoring it, of course. Some of it was a bit strong for a sensitive girl.

'Yes,' she said, 'that fits the pattern. We're all debenture holders. When I was president of the Club, I tried to get some back. Nobody wanted to let go of them. They're almost priceless now. I know who owns them all, and how much. If you want to get the Club by the throat, that's where the throat is. We own it.'

'Nobody's been after you?'

'They're afraid of me. Harris said somebody in a Ferrari or something came around. Wanted to see the dahlias. Harris told him to buy a ticket. But first, wait a few months till they start to bloom. Another one got over the wall. I'm afraid he'll be frightfully sore for a week or so. You're the only one who can get to the bottom of this, Don Joevanni. For the same reason I refuse to let you come near me.'

'So I noticed.' I squeezed her.

'Well, a friendly squeeze is all right. The Lordleigh maiden who owns the most debentures is –'

'I thought it was you.'

'I'm the second most. The one who owns the most is the most dangerous of all. Could she be the one who is trying to corner a controlling interest? It's Louisa. I had trouble getting her into the Club.'

'Because she's black.'

'Maybe she's a quarter black. She has a gorgeous all-year tan. Her daddy, the Empire-builder, was white as a snowball, and her mum was a lovely milk-chocolate. Beautiful, too. Louisa's probably richer than I am. Rhodesia, now Zimbabwe, copper, mountains of it, and a huge multi-national. Anyway, she's got more debentures. Really, I don't need to tell *you* about Louisa.'

'Best topspin lob at the Club.'

'I remember the time that Billy Swan and I knocked you two out of the semi-finals of the mixed.'

'But you and I could have beaten anyone, luv. As Peter Flemming would have put it, the best mixed pair in the Club is Tish and anybody.'

'I wasn't talking about tennis.'

'I was.'

'Let's skip over your pure, brother-and-sisterly relationship with Louisa, St Joseph.'

'Let's, little sister.' I squeezed her again, a brotherly squeeze. 'You have to remember, Louisa is an animal lover, above all. She loves animals more than people.'

'And she thinks of you as an animal.'

'That's unfair, but it *is* true. I *am* an animal, and so are you. You're just putting the wrong spin on it.'

'You're certainly the most animal I know, Jo-Jo.'

'Or the second most.'

'Let's not get political,' she said.

'You're the most animal *I* know. Shall we rut, primate?'

'A dry rut?' she asked.

'If that's all you've got going.'

'You're a bare-headed tail-feathered cockerel, Jo-Jo, your Latin name is *horrendus bastardus*.'

Tish and I were both laughing. We could never be dead serious for long. And sex is always a hair's breadth away from loony farce, the Almighty's raunchiest slapstick, whacking the human race in its tenderest places.

'Let's not get sentimental, Joey. We're talking about Louisa. And I know several yachtsmen who think of Louisa as a crocodile, a black nigger croc. They would like to skin her and make a crocodile briefcase, or filofax. (*That's British for a kind of yuppy pocket notefile*.) Do you realize what she did to their yacht club?'

'It was environmental. She saw it as a great quivering chunk of ecology. Colour her green.'

'She took a perfectly beautiful yacht club and turned it into a mud hole.'

'She had already bought it with her own money, and she turned it *back* into a mud hole. She gave it back to its original owners, the red-breasted chiselbills, the only place in this hemisphere, practically, where they can mate, and nest, and make more wittle chisels. Have you been there lately, and heard their happy lyrical coos?'

'You're the wrong man for this job, Jo-Jo. You're on the side of the enemy, a golden tan crocodile shaped like a showgirl.'

'You're not being fair to her, Tishia. Do you want to change these islands into a concrete jungle?'

'Do you want the Lordleigh Club turned into a refuge for water buffaloes?'

'Is that what she has in mind?'

'I don't *know* what she has in mind. I haven't spoken to her since she turned the Saxon Yacht Club into a bird-cage. I know she has definitely talked to Mabel about getting together for some kind of meeting. And Mabel is a big debenture holder.'

'You really feel Louisa's behind all this Ferrari stuff?'

'Well, she could buy Ferraris like popcorn.'

'You're serious? She's trying to get a quorum of debenture holders to turn the Club into a mud hole?'

'I don't know. That's why I asked you to dinner, Jo-Jo. It may be a matter of life or mud.'

'That was the only reason?'

'The only reason. I can't help it if you add more reasons. Please, Joey.'

'Okay, little sister. Incidentally, I still love you. I just can't stand you.'

'Out, now.'

I kissed her, on the forehead. 'See you sometime, luv.'

'Bring your own mud.'

I think Harris was disappointed. All he said, of course, was 'Good-night, Sir,' as he opened the huge wrought-iron gates of Mountvale Park, but I thought I detected a note of sadness. Harris must have known we couldn't have done anything definitive in that much time. And why hadn't I stayed for breakfast?

Then, as I drove through he said, as an afterthought, 'Strange that you should leave the door of your car open, sir.'

'I'd never do that, Harris.'

'I found it open, sir. I closed it, of course. Looked a bit like rain.'

'Thank you, Harris.'

Why would anyone do that? Of course you can open a car door very quietly, but it's hard to close it without making a noise. You'd just leave it open, wouldn't you?

# *Eleven*

The old Porsche wanted her head, and I gave it to her, but responsibly. There was almost nobody on the road. Most of the British go to bed early. Or back to the telly. But we must have set some kind of rally record between Mountvale and Chelsea. I crowded in close enough to Subby's garage to avoid being wheel-clamped, and used my key on her door. Not a sound, only a tiny night-light on. Even a slight, ladylike snore.

I took off every stitch, popped into her loo for a few seconds, and then snugged in with Subby, who never wore a thing in bed and was already facing more or less in the right direction. Lovely, nice sleepy-clean smell.

'Who is it, quick, without thinking?' I said.

'Mmmmmm,' too sleepy for jokes. 'Back in a second, darling.'

And she was. We were just holding each other closely, very closely, for enough minutes. Mouths together, no dialogue.

First words, from Subby: 'Well, big bomb. Short fuse. Thereby hangs a tale?'

'No tales till breakfast. Busy evening.'

'You're telling *me*, sonny boy.'

'Night night, luv.'

But she made sure to re-set the digits on her radio

alarm twenty minutes earlier than breakfast, to give us time for a friendly little encore.

Subby had an editorial meeting that morning, so breakfast and conversation had to be brief. She was doing a juggling act, simultaneously making us porridge (*oatmeal to you*) with dark brown sugar and cinnamon, popped into the microwave for four minutes, and orange juice and coffee, while she was doing a miracle slap-up for a fancy meeting. The object was to end up terribly smart. (*'Smart' in British has nothing to do with your brain, only your looks.*) But she did know I had been going to the big Tish Do, because I had told her.

At this stage hair and eyes and all that were done, and she was in a pretty silk slip, looking lovely, and we were eating our breakfast.

'But I can tell, Joey, you're still in love with Tish. Aren't you?'

'I'm in love with you, Subby.' That with a coffee cup in my hand, looking even smarter than usual, since I was black tie from the waist down, and an open white shirt from the waist up.

'You didn't answer the question.'

'It's academic, luv. Not part of the world. You're the real world. That's what I came back to. Real bed, real Subby, real love, real wonder.'

You can't tell a woman that you can love two women at the same time. But you can. Even if you can't stand one of them.

'But I can certainly tell you didn't, Joe. In any other real bed.'

'Of course you can, and I didn't. I'm your steady boyfriend. Mono-Joe.'

'Okay, Mono-Joe. But you were jolly well tempted, sonny boy.'

'Temptation is everywhere lassie. That's what character is for.'

'Hummph. Pardon me while I slip on a suit.'

She did, a beautifully tailored one, with a crisp white blouse. She looked, as only Subby can, formal, cool and teribly sexy all at the same time. Not as beautiful as Tish, or as Gwenny used to be. But who is?

'I've got the car, crowding your garage. I'll drop you at the office.'

She usually walked over to the South Kensington tube. No problem driving to her office, just a few minutes away, but parking within miles was impossible.

When I got out of the car, at home, in Madeleine's driveway, she couldn't help noticing I was wearing black tie without a tie and carrying the jacket. Being Madeleine, she didn't even raise an eyebrow.

'Oh, good-morning Joseph. How was Tish?'

'Fine, Madeleine. She sent you her regards. Fascinating evening. I'll tell you all about it.'

'I have something to tell you, Joseph. I could be sure I heard someone in your flat last night. It's right over my bedroom, you know.'

(Yes, I did know, dammit. I often told some of my little friends to take off their high heels.)

'Really?' I said.

'I was going to call the police. Then I thought you might have come back.'

'I didn't.'

'Oh, I am worried about you, Joseph. There must be some very dangerous people about.'

So when I got upstairs, I looked around. People who live with computers don't leave many papers around. But I did notice that my mouse, attached to the computer by a thin cable, had been pulled over to the other side. Some very sophisticated character must have been there. Reading my hard disk? I do keep a journal on it. Was somebody interested in the detective work I was doing?

# *Twelve*

I phoned Louisa at her Surrey rain forest, and just got a funny noise. Was she keeping her phone in the mud, too? I remembered that Tish said Mabel had been in touch with her, so I phoned Mabel. I had to look up the number, it had been so long ago.

'Well, Josie, old mate, what happened to you?' she said.

I just said I wanted to find Louisa.

'So do I, luv. I can't get her on the phone. In fact, I'd rather not, I think my phone is being tapped, especially in the Louisa department. When you're out this way, pop in. Bring your weeding and your fucking clothes, Josie, and you can choose which.'

That 'especially in the Louisa department' made me so curious I drove out there right away. Mabel lived in St George's Hill, one of the fanciest residential areas south-west of London. You had to have at least an acre of land, and many people had more than that. A lot of them were so rich they belonged to both the St George's tennis club and Lordleigh. St George's is gorgeous, but they have tennis and squash only. Their golf is about a mile away.

Her place was completely surrounded by rhododendrons, about thirty feet high, just like the ones Gwenny and I used to have. In fact it was right next door, and that was what started the whole trouble.

I drove right past our old place, almost invisible from the road behind all the bushes. They had changed the name. I came around the corner and drove in between Mabel's shrubs. The house, like ours, was mostly red brick with lots of gables, probably an imitation of the famous Lutyens country houses. Before I had even set the hand brake, Mabel came waddling out. She must have gained at least three stone. (*A 'stone' is the only way the English talk about human weight. It means fourteen pounds, and is always used in the singular, stone not stones.*)

'Where have you been, Josie? I haven't seen you for years.'

'I've been at the club, Mabel. Where have you been?'

'I got too fat for tennis. I've been bowling.'

In a big club like Lordleigh, you mostly see the people who play the same game. The bowling green is in back of the stables. You might not see a bowler once a year.

'Which are those, your weeding or your fucking clothes, Josie?'

I was in jeans. I said, 'Neither one. I gave up both.' Actually I never liked that word. It made sex sound dirty. In fact, Mabel was lucky to get into Lordleigh at all. It was a mistake. She was what the British call rich working class, and she got into the Club by putting on a fake-posh accent, and then it was too late. Of course she could sound fake-posh any time she wanted.

She put her arms around me and gave me a wet kiss. Mabel thought sex was funny, which of course it often is, but for her it was funny all the time. 'You really giving up fucking, Josie? You're famous for it. Move over and make room for me in the front seat. I've always wanted to fuck you in your Porsche.'

'You did already.'

'Not in the Porsche. Everywhere else, mate.'

She never put on the posh for me. I was a Yank, and Yanks didn't buy the system, which made us seem to be on her side, because for her the system was bad. She was rich because her Dad had owned a big string of pubs.

I knew she was kidding, and didn't have the slightest intention of having sex with me anymore. In fact, you can't do it in my car, not with a woman in her weight class. And for anybody who has a bed, a car is simply dumb.

I could almost cry about the way Mabel looked. She was once a genuine bimbo, a buxom, slightly bleached blonde, her boobs practically fighting to get out, and the rest of her plump, but luscious, not fat. Her clothes always looked tight. She was never my type at all, from a loving standpoint, but you have to remember my condition at that early time. I was still wildly in love with Gwenny, who was more affectionate with me than with a cuddly puppy. But she was sick then, and getting worse. We hadn't had sex for more than a month, and that was a very gentle nothing, I was so afraid I might hurt her.

Back at that time, I didn't dare even to *look* at Mabel, and luckily we couldn't see over the bushes. On that day, *the* day you might say, I was out with a machete chopping at the bracken, an English weed that looks like a fern. It was hot and I had on jeans and tennis shoes and no shirt.

I managed to trip over a root and went down into a wild holly bush, with leaves like little razors. And there I was, lying on the ground, sweaty and with bloody scratches. When I tried to get up, I discovered my ankle was sprained and I couldn't stand on it. I went down again, and yelled, *God dammit!* I was on the ground looking as though I had been murdered, and in came Mabel, from her side of the rhododendrons. She had nothing on but cut-off jeans and a tight T-shirt, with the nipples showing through like little bumps.

'Ohmygod, Josie, who did it to you?'

'I did it to myself, Mabel.'

Of course we knew each other well. We had played tennis together, and had the usual neighbourly mishmash.

'Can you get up, luv? Let me help you.'

At this stage she was a hundred per cent motherly, helping a hurt kid.

'It's my ankle.'

'Here, lean on me, luv.'

I hobbled back with her to her kitchen, a nice, expensive kitchen with an Aga coal stove. She sat me down on a wooden chair and washed off the sweat and blood. The cuts were very small.

'I think you may live, Josie.' She put on three small Band-aids. I still remembered my first week in England when I cut myself and went into a drug store, which is called a chemist's, and asked, 'What is the English word for Band-aid?' The man said Band-aid, and he had some. So I guessed I was in a friendly country.

'I'll kiss it and make it well.' She did, she kissed one of the bandages, and it was still motherly. Then she raised her mouth up to about my lip level, and that was when I think something in her snapped.

Who knows, it is entirely possible that something in *me* snapped at the same time. It was certainly not *all* her fault. And not all my fault either. It started as a hurt-kid kiss, and who was responsible for the escalation? Who took it further? All I know, factually, is that it went from a hurt-kid kiss to a big-kid kiss in about three seconds, and after that everybody in the room was taking a whooping big part in the exercise.

You can't do everything with a sprained ankle, but there are some things you can still do.

For just sheer power-passion I think Mabel had it over anybody, even Tish. It was like one of those high-tech explosions that takes a whole building down in one shot. She had a nice, clean vinyl floor, coloured red, and she had the advantage of knowing that nobody else was home. I didn't know anything except that I seemed to be mixed up in a whole crowd of highly pneumatic sex maniacs, and I'm not implying that I didn't enjoy it, or add to the hooligan riot. I had a ball. And there is absolutely no question that she did, as well.

I would like to add here that, at this point in time, as the fellow said, I had not even really kissed any other woman since I first made love to Gwenny, a kid, and umpteen years before. I never wanted to.

'Ohmygod, luv,' she said when we were through, and practically out of breath. 'I didn't mean to do that.'

'I didn't either, Mabel.'

'But smashing, right?' Big smile.

'Bloody smashing,' I said. (*Note to Americans:* bloody *is a really dirty word in British; nobody understands why, since the word blood is perfectly OK. Nice old ladies will practically faint if you say 'bloody'. One theory is that it's a contraction of 'by 'er lady', and maybe they weren't talking about the lady's head. Just remember not to say it to a nice old grandma;*)

There was no way I could ever be in love with Mabel, or anything even close. But I had to admit to myself that this was the first real ding-dong lay I had had in years.

I assumed that this was just a normal bang-up for Mabel. Maybe every day with the milkman, but that was not so. Mabel was just as starved as I was. I knew she was divorced, but at that time I didn't know the real facts. I had seen her husband, of course. He was as handsome a man as I'd ever met. Absolutely beautiful, and also fake-posh. Mabel must have gone head over heels, and made the mistake of marrying him without trying him out first. And yet, as she explained to me later, he was absolutely stone cold. He wasn't gay, he wasn't anything. He didn't want to do it with anybody, not even guys. Finally, she divorced him. The money was hers. I'm sure she had had *affaires*, but the point I'm making is that Mabel had been on that day just as sex-starved as I was. We were both bombs all primed to go off.

I said, 'I have to get back, Mabel. I can't leave Gwenny for too long.'

'How is she, Josie?'

'Very sick.'

'Let me know if I can help, luv.'

She loaned me an old walking-stick, and I limped back. Gwenny was sick in bed, and I told her I had fallen down, and that Mabel had helped me.

'That was nice of her, Joey. She's very good-hearted.'

It would never have occurred to Gwenny that any such thing had happened. And it never had before and didn't again, until after she died. And after that I think it was just Mabel's hurt-kid syndrome coming into action once more. After Gwenny, when I was simply smashed up, Mabel felt sorry for me, and we had a good family-type *affaire*, plus a nice pot-luck dinner together, once in a while, sitting cozy and warm in her kitchen, alongside the Aga. And we talked about Gwenny, and how much I had loved her. Once Mabel even cried. I realized, again, how glorious passionate sex could be, even with Mabel. It was probably the thing that started me off, on my wicked afterlife.

Mabel gave me one affectionate squeeze in my Porsche, and we went back to her garden.

'You know, Josie, it was good in the long run, that thing we had together, way back. You never really loved me, but you needed me then, after Gwenny, and I needed it too. It showed me how good it could be, to have a nice, friendly bloke in your bed, and it still is, with Jacko.' She had married some fellow in the bowling, and they were apparently happy. And I finally sold the house and moved into my little flat at Madeleine's.

'You don't mind if I keep on weeding, do you, luv? I don't think Antonio is going to show up, again.'

'You still have Antonio, do you?' She used to have a wild Italian gardener.

'He still can't understand why anybody should grow flowers instead of vegetables. Who eats flowers?'

'Give me a fork and a rubber mat. I can still weed.'

We kneeled down side by side.

'Tell me about Louisa,' I said. 'Is she planning to do something crazy about the Club?'

'You know Louisa.'

'Did she ever ask you how many debentures you have?'

'Yes. I told her.'

'When?'

'A few weeks ago.'

'Did she say why?'

'Well, she said if the debenture ladies all got together we could do anything we wanted with the Club. She thought we might have a meeting, and decide.'

'Did she mention specifically anything about water buffaloes?'

'Water who?'

'Buffaloes.'

'Not to me. All she said was that anything was possible. Maybe you'd better talk to her, luv. You know what she did to that yacht club. If you're going to weed, Josie, you've got to get out the roots.'

'Is this better?'

'And lean over closer this way, luv. It reminds me. We did have a hell of a lot of good fucking together, didn't we?'

# Thirteen

Mabel had me so scared I decided to drive right to Louisa's rain forest. Well, it was as close to a rain forest as you can have in Southern England. To any Yank, the first winter in England seems like a long Fall. You may get one inch of snow the whole time, but it's never really cold, like an American winter. You'll never need a storm coat, just a warm raincoat. Look at a global map, and you can't believe it. You're as far north as Hudson Bay.

But in her rain forest, the outdoor part, Louisa could grow no mangoes, no coconuts, no bananas, and monkeys can catch cold outdoors here. But Louisa was doing the best she could to stop the greenhouse effect.

When I drove into Louisa's jungle I wished I had my old machete back again. The leaves were swishing against the side of my car. I went over a bridge with bamboo railings. On both sides was a kind of everglade swamp. Louisa told me once there were no crocodiles in it, but she wouldn't advise swimming. I heard the scream of a peacock, and I saw a multi-coloured flappitty flap go by overhead, definitely something else. I could swear that a slimey whatsit slithered around to the other side of a tree.

I rumbled over one of those cattle grid things that cows won't walk over, and drove to a sprawling mansion that looked like something out of the white highlands – or is it lowlands? – of what used to be Rhodesia, wide overhanging roof and a screened front porch. Metal window screens are as rare as giraffes in England because normally they aren't needed.

Louisa came bursting out of the front door. She was wearing a kind of denim sarong, and in the first few moments, nothing on above the waist, since she was putting on a plaid shirt, a MacDonald plaid, her father's. That was her name, of course, MacDonald. But until it was buttoned up I could see her lovely golden-tan breasts. I rushed to meet her, and we put our arms around each other and kissed, a full-blooded animal kiss, very sexy but not intended to lead to anything else. This was no stone-age kid, of course, she had degrees from both Vassar and Sussex. She still talked with that funny, flat accent the whites have in Zimbabwe and South Africa.

'Oh, Joey, you're my favourite animal. Where have you been, darling?'

I was still holding her very close, looking into those big, beautiful dark brown eyes. 'Well, for one thing, Lulu, I've been trying to get you on the phone.'

'Oh, I think I've got it back on the hook now. Can you keep a secret, darling?'

'You know damned well I can.'

'I've just got back from Southampton. I was girl-running.'

'Who?'

'Phoebe. I don't think you know her.'

'Is she a member of the Club?'

'Only a social member, I believe. She just blew up the fur department at Harrods. Animal rights, you know.'

'And you've been hiding her?'

'It doesn't do any good to send her to jail. She'd just come out and blow it up again. She's an idealist. I've been re-educating her. I've switched her to whales. I read her a wonderful poem, *Whale Nation*, written by that fabulous hippy who, somebody told me, got thrown out of Eton. Williams?'

'Heathcote (*Hethcut*) Williams, I think.'

'It made her cry. I just came back from putting her on a Greenpeace boat. I told them she's a little girl who's in love with a dolphin. The captain is a pal of mine. I haven't forgotten the fur people. I'm trying to persuade Princess Di to model another fake fur, maybe in Chinese red, and say, again, "It's all right, it's a fake." Much more effective than bombs. Phoebe has promised me: no more setting fire to butcher shops or liberating chimpanzees.'

'I want to talk to you about the Club.'

'Later, darling. My part is a secret. I have to go up to the barley acres now. Molly needs me. Come along.'

'It's important. I have to talk to you this minute.'

'There's always the chance you could worm it out of me, Joey. I dare you to try. Kiss me again, darling. You make me feel sexy. Remember when we were sleeping up in the mud together?'

'I'm not here for that, Lulu.'

'You always take sex so seriously, Joey. What is one man and one woman, doing a totally fake birth-pill biological charade, just for fun, compared with a whole terribly endangered planet?'

'I'm not talking about sex. You are.'

'To say nothing of millions of unfairly treated animals. I'm leaving right now. You can wait here for me. I have a new boa constrictor you could play with.'

'Just answer me one thing, Lulu. Do you have any plans for water buffaloes?'

'No, but it is an idea. They can be quite lovely. I knew one once.' She walked over to her Range Rover and opened the door. 'I'm going to count to three, Joey. Do you want to choose between me and a snake? One! Two!'

She sat in the driver's seat and started the motor.

'Three!'

She moved it about yard and would have left if I hadn't made a dive for the left-hand door.

'I thought that would bring you around. Fasten your seat-belt, darling.' We were already zooming across her bamboo bridge. 'As a matter of fact, you should be fascinated by the story of Molly and the oasis. Maybe you and Maxie could do a Disney on it. And it's a lovely ride.'

We headed north for more than an hour, with all the apples and bananas we could eat. And every time I mentioned the Lordleigh Club she changed the subject. She was every bit as dictatorial as Tish, and with just as much power, but no *snap*.

'I'll tell you a story, Joey. Once upon a time, there was a beautiful piece of English countryside. There were ten lovely fields, each one surrounded by a hedgerow, and each of these hedges was full of life. There were hedgehogs and rabbits and foxes, and pheasants and partridges, and nesting birds. There was a pond with little fish, and frogs. There were meadows sown with wild grasses, like crested dogstail, and meadow fescue, and cocksfoot, and pretty wild flowers like cowslip and foxglove. There were fine English trees like oak and chestnut, rowan and ash and maple, and lime, to say nothing of lovely shrubs, like wild privet, and hazel, and holly, and guelder rose. Have another banana, Joey.'

'Thank you, Lulu.'

'The story isn't over. Some big men came with bulldozers. They ripped out the hedges and the trees and the bushes, and filled in the pond. Then they sprayed the land with chemical fertilizers, and herbicides and pesticides until it was a great brown fifty acre plain, and all life was extinct, all the insects and birds and rabbits and frogs and butterflies were dead. Then they brought in big machines and planted winter barley, over every single inch. During the course of all this, a determined little lady named Molly Jones, who had once lived on the land in question, made a Molotov cocktail out of a Pepsi-cola bottle full of petrol, lit it, and threw it at the bulldozer. Well, she missed, but they had her up before a local magistrate, who asked her if she was sorry. She said she was sorry she missed. That's how I heard about her. If I hadn't put up bail, she'd have gone to jail. We had a long talk, and I told her I agreed with her in principle, but even if she burned down the bulldozer, they were insured anyway, and they would buy a new one, and she would get five years in the pokey.

'Well, there was another piece of about five acres alongside, mostly a junk lot full of rusty cars, and the bulldozer men were going after that, too, but I got in ahead of them and bought it. I told Molly we would make an oasis, and bring back the animals. That was a few years ago. We'll be there pretty soon, Joey.'

We drove in alongside the field of barley.

'See for yourself, Joey. Everything is dead.'

'The barley isn't dead.'

'There's no use being sentimental. It's intensive farming, and they're just adding to the barley mountain.'

Then we saw the sign, 'M. Jones, Garden Centre.'

'It doesn't have to make money, but we're just about breaking even now.'

We drove up near the greenhouse, and Molly came out, smiling. She was skinny and about five feet high, wearing overalls.

'See what I brought you, Molly.'

The whole back end of Lulu's wagon was full of plants.

Molly opened the tailgate, and said, 'Oh, that's lovely, Louisa. Let me get those right into the glasshouse and water them.'

'Fine. I'll wander around and see how things are growing. Come along, Joey.'

I followed her.

'You see, the animals are already coming back.'

'I don't see any.'

'That's because you don't know how to look. Already I can smell that some foxes have been by here last night.'

'I can see all the young saplings.'

'Yes, that's a baby oak, and that's an ash, and that one's a chestnut.'

'How can you tell?'

'By the leaves, darling. You see that flutter down on the meadow? That's a partridge. And that little hole down there is where the badgers live, and over there, in a burrow, is a family of weasels. You see all those butterflies?'

'That I can see.'

'They're flying around that guelder rose, the snowball tree. The butterflies like the pretty white flowers. And how many butterflies do you see around the Club?'

'Not many.'

'Not any. It's all that spraying that kills them. We're definitely going to change that. When we get control.'

I turned on her, like an avenging angel. 'Aha! I've got you now. A confession!'

'You mean that I'm planning to get control of the Club? Of course, darling. They're being very naughty. Some of them will have to be spanked.'

'And what will be the result of that? Mud?'

'If that's what they need, Joey. Ecology is very complicated.'

'And that's why you want all those debentures?'

'Oh, goodness, I have as many as I need.'

'And that's why you're getting in touch with Mabel, and Joanna, and Tish, and —'

'They all have debentures, Joey. It's democratic, like an election.'

'I think we've got to have a long talk, Lulu.'

'Oh, good, darling, the longer the better. Maybe we should go up to the mud and bring our sleeping-bag. You'll see what a big improvement there is now. Are you still paying attention? Here is Molly's tree nursery, and over there are the shrubs. And she has bedding plants by the thousand. We're showing the people around here all kinds of pretty new things.'

We saw it all, and it was becoming very ecological, all right, though a barley eater, or drinker, might have a different point of view. There were no cages for animals. They could go wherever they liked.

We said goodbye to Molly on the way out.

'These plants are absolutely smashing, Louisa. I can take cuttings, and split roots, and I haven't even got into the seeds.'

'I'm sending you a lot more of those. Be good now, Molly.'

As we rolled out, I said, 'I'm not through with you, Lulu.'

'I certainly hope not, darling. I had them put in a nice picnic basket, for me, but it's usually enough for two or three people, and any animals who are passing by. And there's a lovely little waterfall almost on the way back. But only if you promise not to mention the Club for at least two hours.'

Nobody else was there. Nobody without four-wheel drive could have made it. We were sitting on a nice sleeping-bag, close to the splashing water. Lulu took off her plaid shirt and she was so gorgeous that it used up all the character I had left to keep my hands, and my lips, to myself. We were eating all kinds of delicious things, mostly vegetarian, like avocado sandwiches and devilled eggs, and Jewish rye bread and sour pickles, and Brie and Camembert cheese, and cashew nuts, and fresh figs, and a luscious red wine.

When we were all finished, and lying side by side on the sleeping-bag, she leaned over and kissed me sweetly on the lips.

'Mmm, that was nice, Joey. It would be very easy to seduce you now. Would you like me to try? I'll do that again.' She pinned down my arms and really gave me one, a long one. She moved her hand down to my jeans, barely touching. But she did leave it there.

'Aha! Definitely signs of life! You are still an animal, Joey. And I think I can take you any time I want.' She laughed a pretty, musical laugh. 'Whatever could I do with you, darling?' Her hand was still lying there, not moving at all. 'There are a number of possibilities.'

'No please, Lulu.'

'Say pretty please.'

I could still feel her hand, and she kissed me again.

'Pretty please, Lulu.'

'Then you must be in love, darling.'

'Yes.'

She moved her hand away. 'Then why didn't you say so, Joey? You know about swans? Absolutely monogamous, they say. I never quite pictured you as a swan, darling. But don't be selfish. Just give me a lovely kiss, and while you're about it, kiss these, in a friendly way.'

'You can't kiss those in a friendly way.'

There was speckled sunlight, filtering through wavy leaves, on her beautiful breasts. But I kissed them just the same, and she made a lovely moan, almost like humming.

'Aren't animals wonderful, Joey? Don't stop, darling. Remember the day of the romantic mud? Don't answer me. That would be a waste of your lovely lips. Just remember.'

I could never forget those early days with Lulu. I was crazy with love for her then. We were thrown together in a mixed tournament, and I was almost frightened of her. I had heard she was so rich, and I could see she was exotic, like a legendary princess. She'd had a frightful marriage with one of the white farmers. He'd had a huge plantation, and when the blacks got independence, he couldn't come to terms with the black government, and he and Lulu fought about that, and about animals, and everything else and she divorced him, and came to England.

She bought her rain forest from another animal fanatic who couldn't afford to keep it up. She was enlarging it when I first saw her. I wondered whether I could ever really approach such a golden princess.

I needn't have worried. After one of our matches, she suggested we stop by her place, and I followed her out in my car.

Lulu brought me into her conservatory, a year-round tropical forest under glass. Here there were real date palms, and banana and mango trees, and tropical flowers, and orchids, and live monkeys.

Best of all was a lovely swimming-pool, almost hidden in greenery, like a swimming hole in a jungle, but with crystal clear water.

'How about a swim?' she said.

'I don't have a suit with me.'

She laughed. 'I don't either.'

'But you're home.'

She laughed, that lovely little-girl tinkle, almost a giggle. 'Take it off, Joey. Last one in's a skinnydipper.' Could a girl learn that at Vassar?

I took off everything, no way to avoid it. And when I looked up, there she was, living gold and not a stitch.

It was the first time I had seen Lulu, all together. As I think back, now, the only sight that compared with this was Tish in the golden lycra, but Lulu's gold was alive. She looked me up and down, laughed, and gave me a push. I splashed in, and heard another splash nearby.

I was almost shy, floating in water as clear as air. Should I face the other way? Should I pretend she wasn't there? I turned slightly, and stared into poolside greenery.

I felt a hand on one shoulder, from behind. And then a hand on the other shoulder, also from behind.

'About face!' she ordered, and spun me around, and then there was pure gold all the way down my front, and she was laughing, and her arms were around me and she was kissing me on the lips. All in all, Lulu was the most uninhibited woman I ever knew.

'Look at the lovely animal I've brought home. Whatever shall I do with it?'

'What you will, ma'am."

'I must treat it kindly. What would you like the most, animal? How about this?' She did a mermaid's bump. 'Or this?' Can a mermaid grind? Well, Lulu could. 'Would you like to have music?' There was a white string, hanging down from a cluster of tropical flowers. All English bathrooms have white strings, no switches allowed. Of course not, the electricity is more than twice as strong, 240 volts. You could kill yourself, with wet hands. Lulu splashed over and pulled the string. Presto! Tango! 'Sorry, you have no choice. A waltz comes on later.'

We did the most erotic water tango I have ever danced, if that's the right word, and then a waltz that coloured the Blue Danube shocking pink.

We started in the water, which solves the weight problem of sex, and was lovely, and we finished up on a bouncy rubber mat, doing an erotic *coda*, which certainly had its points, but was much too fast, almost like riding a bolting horse.

'Oh, Joey, Joey, I am so glad you have become an animal. I loved it, I did love it. Did you?'

'I love you, Lulu, you are simply golden-gorgeous. You are definitely worth teaching.'

'*Teaching?*' It was almost an animal howl.

'You're like a natural swimmer who has swum all her life, but she'll never win any races.'

'Oh, you mean my swimming?'

'Yes, I could make that much faster but I'm not talking about swimming, I'm talking about lovemaking. What a terrible waste of pleasure.'

'Oh, Joey. I thought it was so nice.'

'It was nice, I just mean it could be nicer. I sometimes wonder if animals really enjoy it at all, surely not half as much as they could. Much too quick, they don't really *savour* it.'

'I'm going to cry.'

'Not yet, darling. You just don't know how much you're missing. You're doing runaway loving. The first lesson will be this evening, in a proper bed. I'll teach you everything I know. I'll double your pleasure, and double it again. And of course that will double mine, too.'

'Really?'

'I promise, if you promise to do what I say.'

She sniffled. 'Can I cry just a little now?'

'Yes, it's a good idea.'

She cried, just a little. And then she smiled, a really beautiful smile, with the world's prettiest teeth.

'Really, twice as much pleasure?'

'Six times as much.' A lie, of course, but in the interests of selling, you have to lie a little.


We ate our feast that evening under glass, in the jungle. Lulu had a marvellous cook, originally from the Dutch East Indies, who gave us his speciality, the rice table, heaven knows how many rice dishes, with a dozen different exotic sauces, and a rice wine. There were tropical fruits, mangoes and passion fruit and kiwis, and melons, most of them home-grown.

'And now,' Lulu said, 'before you give me your lesson I'm going to give you one. I am going to teach you how to love the mud.'

'Impossible. I hate mud.'

'This is more than mud, it's stinking mud.'

'No, not even for you, Lulu.'

'It's an acquired stink, like learning to like olives, or oysters.'

'Never.'

'Come up to my study. I'll show you.'

We went into the main house and up to her study, one entire wall of which was an aquarium, so full of brightly coloured tropical fish that it looked like a painting in motion.

'I'll tell you all about them later, Joey. Now we're talking about mud. Here is an Ordnance Survey of the yacht club area.'

The British have made hundreds of maps of every minute area, in a scale so large that individual buildings and trees are visible. You could probably see the people if they'd hold still long enough.

'This is a tidal estuary, always an ecological battleground. Here is the yacht club. They have put in this dam, which has flooded all the mud that was there with dirty water. And that flooded area is now their marina, with a lock, there. So now the only mud that isn't flooded is here. That's where we're going, tomorrow.'

'What if I won't go?'

'You have no choice, Joey. You are now my mate, animal-speaking. Right?'

'Right.'

'So, you come under the rules of animal rights –'

Always beware of fast-talking women.

'Well –'

'And, as my mate, you are going to the mud, tomorrow. The subject is closed. And now, whenever you are ready, I'm at your service, for further mate-training.'

She smiled, an autocratic smile, of course, somewhat like Tish's, in fact. But still, without the *snap*. The reason I obeyed Lulu at this point was that I simply could not resist her.

And, a bit later on, when we were warmed to it,

mate-wise, we began the tutorials. We went to the great bed in her orchid bedroom. It took me back to the days of Doreen, in the old brownstone, in Manhattan, so many years before. There are dozens of little *pas de deux* in lovemaking, as in ballet, that are physical, body movements, which can be either clumsy, or beautiful, and, at their best, incredibly rewarding.

'You see what I mean, darling? Much slower, more loving, more caring, and a little bit more of a throb, like this. Doesn't that feel better?'

'Oh yes, yes, Joey, do that again!'

'You have to do it, too.'

'Yes, darling.'

'And never, never hurry.'

But it didn't save me from the mud. We reviewed a few of our special exercises the next morning, but not for long.

'Up, up, Joey, the mud is calling. We're leaving right after breakfast. You have a choice of canoes; kayaks, dug-outs or Indian.'

'Oh, Indian, if you mean Red Indian. I'm an old Indian canoeman.'

'Navahoe?'

'No, I'm from Cherokee country, in Missouri. We used to shoot the rapids in the Meramec River. But not a birchbark job.'

'Mine is alu-MIN-ee-um,' she said, pronouncing it the British way.

'I'm used to wood and canvas, but aluminium's OK.'

We loaded it on top of her wagon and put camping equipment in the car. Then we drove about an hour, mostly south-west, staying near the channel. We parked close to the shore.

'You see, we're on the other side of the estuary. My bit of mud is over there, not far from the yacht club.'

We loaded our canoe with a light tent, a big sleeping-bag and food. I put Lulu in the front seat and, wearing light sneakers and shorts for wading, I pushed us out and jumped into the rear seat. I began paddling, and so did Lulu, up front. I remembered what we used to call the 'Indian stroke', ending each stroke with a quarter turn, so you can do many strokes on the same side.

We could see some of the sails from the Saxon Sailing Club, tacking back and forth. They were all small, and I suspected they were mostly centreboard sailing dinghies. Very nice in a moderate wind. I had one once.

Long before we reached the mud, I could smell it. Unfortunately the wind was coming from that direction.

Do you mind if I draw a discreet curtain over this episode? I can still smell that mud as I write. We did drag our canoe up on to muddy land, on the other side of the sea wall of the yacht club. Lulu began crying almost from the beginning.

'No, no, no, it's not enough.'

'Not enough what?'

'Not enough mud. Thousands of waders depend on it.'

'Waders?'

'Long-legged birds, like dunlin and redshank.'

'I don't see any.'

'They don't *come* now. This is where they stop for the winter, thousands of them. Most of them will die.'

Lulu poked around in the mud all day, and we finally pitched our tent on ground just above the mud.

I remember, late at night, we were lying together in our sleeping-bag.

'Just listen to that, darling,' she whispered. 'Listen to the mud, it's alive.'

I could hear it all right. There was a kind of thin crackling sound.

'You hear? There are millions of tiny, microscopic living things in there, and all related to the salt marshes, and the birds. I never, never should have done it.'

'Done what?'

'Allowed the yacht club to lease the land.'

So she owned the whole thing, and that was when she decided to let it go back to mud, and be a home for ten thousand birds. She did help the yacht club to find a new place, but many of the sailors never forgave her. And in spite of Lulu, I never learned to love the mud, not even when I thought I should.

And that's what I was day-dreaming about, lying beside Lulu, so many years later, and in the midst of such lovely scenery, near and far, even including a waterfall.

'The trouble is, Lulu, that your part about the Club simply doesn't add up. You want to get all the rich women together, so you can do something ecologically violent to it?'

'Sometimes you may have to be violent. Nature is violent. Ecology can be a battle to the death, that's how evolution works. It isn't over, it's still working. Sometimes by being violent, you can help nature to be less violent. Don't you understand, darling?'

'I understand that, but not why you should be sending a beautiful stud to Fiona, or why you should order somebody to break into Joanna's strong-box, or climb over Tish's wall. And why did you send Deirdre a Lamborghini driven by a gigolo with wavy chestnut hair and a classical Greek profile?'

'Joey, I didn't do a single one of those things.'

'Somebody did. Apparently someone wanted to know who really controls the Club.'

'But I know that already. I know all the ladies well. All I have to do is call them up. And I'm going to. But who did all those other things? And what in the world are they trying to do to the Club?'

'Something even worse than what you did to the sailing club?'

'Who knows, Joey? And what could they do to anybody who is snooping around? Don't you realize they could even kill you, if they had to? I would hate to have anything happen to a nice animal like you.'

# *Fourteen*

I did think about Lulu's warning. I'm not the hero type, and I have no desire to mix it with any violent characters. Certainly people were beginning to be interested in what I was doing. Were they the kind of people who shot other people?

On the way back from Lulu's, I could swear somebody in a green car was following me. I mean, intelligently following me, trying to keep out of sight. If it got too close, it dropped back.

Finally, when I was almost to the Club, I just stopped, to see what would happen. I was surprised when the car stopped behind me, and I could see it was an Aston, a beauty, in what we used to call British Racing Green, a dark green. Would a gorgeous stud get out?

No, it was a fat fellow, middle-aged, in a sport coat.

'I thought that would be you, in the old Porsche,' he said, in a London accent, almost a BBC. 'My name is Jones. I didn't want to call you. I think your phone is tapped.'

He didn't look threatening. Not then, anyway. 'It's just business, really. You're at Rambleys, yes?'

'Yes.'

'They might be interested in new business, yes?'

'Why not?' I had nothing to do with that part, of course.

'It could be very big money.'

Well, you have to have very big money to be fooling around with Astons.

'What's it about?'

'It's complicated. Come to see us, and we'll talk.'

He gave me a calling card. Locksleys.

'That's a casino, isn't it?'

'The biggest one. Early in the week?'

'I'm pretty swamped now.' That was the truth. I'd been seeing too many of the ladies. I'd have to be getting more chocolate on my fingers.

'You won't be sorry. I can promise you that.'

He started back to the Aston.

'Nice to talk to you,' he said.

He hadn't fired a single shot. He turned around and drove back in the other direction. I also noticed that a Ferrari came by, going in the same direction I was. Surely there wasn't any connection, was there? Then why should I have that strange, cold, clammy feeling? I drove on to Madeleine's.

I was busy. I meant to go in to Locksleys, just out of curiosity – or was it closer to fear? I also meant to call Fiona. In fact I did, a couple of times, and all I got was her answerphone. And then my phone did ring, and there she was.

She said, 'You know, Jo-Jo darling, I think our answerphones are falling in love with each other. Should we just leave them together? Maybe they'd have a whole litter of little answerphones.'

It was sometimes hard to turn Fiona off. I could never actually reach her personally, and left all kinds of threats, love songs, and gibberish on her tape.

'You mean this is really you, Fifi, and not a recording?'

'In person, darling. You, too? How teddibly lucky we both are. Would you mind breathing heavily, and saying something filthy, and I'll gasp and faint, and you can record a red hot loveybomb.'

'Stop talking, Fifi. Are you alone?' I knew damned well she'd never have called if she hadn't been.

'Well, prcatically, darling. Shall I get rid of him? Run back to your Ferrari, boy. Clap-clap! I really don't have time for you amateurs now, Jo-Jo. When you hear the tone, just repeat your name and telephone number slowly and clearly. *Beeeeeep!* I do really *have* to see you in person, darling, and there isn't a minute to lose.'

'How about a drink at the Club this evening?'

We were at one of the tables near the lake, flowers all around. The sun was beginning to set. And Fifi couldn't stop talking.

'I'm afraid the Ferraris and that gorgeous man were really worth it to them. They were hunting, and they got the dead pigeon they were after. Me, darling, all of me. More of me than they ever *hoped*. Woody practically owns me now, more than he even intended. Now I have to confess he just has to whistle, and I'll come running. I have just now run to you, because he has just whistled and told me to. You've heard of AAs. Well I'm now trying to become a GA, that's Gamblers Anonymous, and that was even more than Woody wanted. He didn't want me, but he's got me, all the same. All he wanted was the Club.'

The problem with Fiona was not to get the truth out of her, but to sort out the truth from all the chatter.

'Could you start over again, Fifi? Who is this Woody who owns you? Even more than you owned me, once upon a time?'

'Who owned who then, Jo-Jo? If it hadn't been for that young scamp, you'd own me still, darling.'

That was an episode I regret. We could make a whole story out of that alone, but not at this moment. I was too fascinated by what Fifi was saying, or not saying, and by the fact that she seemed so disturbed, almost terrified, by *something*. But in a nutshell – shall we have just that? Fifi had a daughter who was almost a Xerox of her mom, a gorgeous body, face a bit angular, dark brown hair. She was just fifteen at the time, and a full-blown woman, even slightly more so than Fifi. Unlike most of the kids in our class-range, who all went to boarding-schools, and were never home, little Feef went to some special local school, and was around. Her father was divorced. She found out about me, and carefully plotted to trick her Mom out of the way so she could slide into Fifi's bed with me, naked, a real nympho-nymphet. She had taken the pill, she said, and her mother would *never* know, and would I please, please make love to her? Maybe I should have spanked her, but I didn't. All my alarm bells were ringing. I could do her great harm by being too tough. I kissed her sweetly, told her she was lovely, which she certainly was, that it was far too soon, and she was far too young, and if she got out of bed immediately, I wouldn't spank her, and I would not tell her mother. She cried a little, but she left. Fifi didn't find out about it until much later, after our *affaire* was over. And little Feef survived, thank God.

'Shall we get back to this man who owns you, Fifi? And makes you shiver the way you're doing right now? His name is Woody? Is he the gigolo fellow?'

'That was just the bait, darling. Even Woody admits he went a little overboard on that, but he thought we were all so teddibly posh that he'd have to go simply screamingly up-market if he was really going to *enslave* us. And dear boy, the one they sent me was – well, Jo-Jo, I hate to say it, but he did make you look like an amateur.'

'Oh, did he?' I knew that Fifi could be cruel, really cruel.

'I wish you could see the look on your face, Jo-Jo. Don't cry, darling, you *are* an amateur. I know you *do* try.'

'I am *not* crying.'

'Your eyes are crying. My dear boy did spoil you for me, darling. Oh my, yes. I can see you're getting too old to be Don Juan. Do you want my hanky?'

'Stop it, Fifi!'

'You might try just a little dab of eye makeup, I can give you some, darling, to put on before you see Woody, and you won't be able to *avoid* that. Someone must have told him that you can simply do *anything* with women. Or make *them* do anything. And that the whole Club is – or was – your own personal harem. I don't think he realizes how old you are!'

If I hadn't been so hugely curious, I think I'd have stood up right then, and walked off. Old? *Me*? But I did wish I had a mirror. Eye makeup? Ridiculous. There was certainly nothing wrong with my eyes. Was there?

'*I* am going to see this Woody?' I said.

'I didn't say that, darling. I said *if* you do. If you have to.'

'Who the hell is Woody, Fifi?'

'You'll find *that* out soon enough, Jo-Jo. All I can tell you now is, Woody just has to say Boo, and I'll Boo. Because now he owns me. And that's why I'm here. All he wants to know is the answer to this question, and I don't even know what the question means. The question is, have you had anything to do with a man who drives a green Aston?'

'The answer is yes. And I'm going to see him again. So what?'

'I don't know what. All I can tell you is, just do what Woody wants and you'll be teddibly glad you did. And if you don't I can promise you, you'll be *fraffly* sorry. All he said was, just put the finger on him, and that's what I'm doing. *Do you feel it, darling?* I'll run along, now, Jo-Jo.'

# *Fifteen*

She did run along, and that one word, yes, is the reason I found myself a forced hostage, wondering whether I would ever have quite the same face again. But I certainly was close to finding the answer to the complicated riddle of the Ferraris, and what was really happening to the ladies of the Lordleigh Club. Whether the suffering was worth it – well, you can be the judge of that. After you've gone through it with me.

The next day was Friday, I'll never forget that. Friday is like no other day in England. It's the jumping-off-to-a-different-life day, when people become different kinds of people, because it's the beginning of the notorious British weekend. For some people it can begin as soon as Friday at 11 am. They leave, and say goodbye to their other life, and hello to the new one.

It was after 4 p.m., and already the traffic jams were beginning to inch out of London. I heard a clattering on Madeleine's back stairs, and immediately afterward a frantic ringing of my bell. I went quickly to open it, and there was Fiona.

'Oh, Jo-Jo, I'm so sorry I put the finger on you. I had to come running to you because I know they've got my phone tapped –'

I put my hand on her shoulder. 'Take it easy, Fifi, it

isn't the end of the world.'

'Well, it could be for you, darling. You don't know Woody, and you don't understand what you did.'

'Do you understand what I did?'

'No, that's the terrifying part of it, Jo-Jo. Don't interrupt! Don't take time to talk. Don't take time to change your clothes. They're coming here for you. Go out right now, and get in your car and start driving, to anywhere. And don't tell me where, they could find out.'

'That's crazy —'

'I parked my car in the Club, so they wouldn't see it parked here. I sneaked over, through the bushes. Now I'm running back.'

She turned and ran down the stairs, calling back, 'Hurry!'

It was like a nightmare. I turned off the Macintosh, threw a sweater over my shoulder, with the sleeves crossed in front, French style, put my wallet, with a credit card in it, in my pocket, along with my keys, and hustled down the stairs to the old Porsche, and drove out of Madeleine's, not even sure where I was going.

Well, I did the best I could. My mistake was stopping at the red light. That was when the two beautiful studs in the red Ferrari spotted me. They pulled up, trying to cut me off — and then I did it, I did a wheel-spinning start, and went *through* the red light, maybe the first time I have ever done that. My old Porsche was nothing like as fast as their car, but at least I was an old hand at mine. I went screaming around a tight curve, and I could see they were right behind. With their car, a really good man could have caught me in seconds. As it was, I kept ahead, in a jolly dramatic car chase (I can't wait to see the movie) for maybe ten minutes, until we came storming into a big construction job, nobody around, but there were about a thousand of those plastic witches' hats all over. I ploughed into the hats, splattering them in all directions, and getting all jammed up. The Ferrari was right on top of me.

Two great big beautiful studs, a lot younger than me, jumped out. They were both still in tennis clothes. One of them opened my car door, which I had forgotten to lock, and said, in a fake-posh accent, 'If you come quietly you won't get hurt.'

'Not now anyway,' the other one said.

They tied my hands behind my back and moved me into the passenger seat in my car. One of them drove mine, and we followed the Ferrari.

'Where are we going?' I asked.

'To a telephone, first.'

We drove around and found a kiosk, but the phone was out of order. We drove around some more. My guy, the one with the curly blond hair, said, 'Ohmygod, we're going to be late.'

'For what?' I asked.

He didn't answer. We found another kiosk, and that phone was out of order, too. The third phone worked. I was sitting with my guardian. The other guy, the one with a slight wave in his blond hair, came back to us. You would have thought he had been sentenced to death.

'What did he say?'

'All I got was his answerphone.'

'Oh, God.'

'Well, it's Friday, and almost five.'

'We never should have played that last set.'

'I left a message. I said we got him.'

'He won't get that until Monday noon at least.'

'So what do we do with him?' He meant me. I remembered that Fiona said something about gambling, and so did the man in the green Aston, and that meant casinos, and everybody knew that could mean Mafia and gangsters. I could wind up with concrete boots, in deep water.

'Well, it has got to be someplace where nobody can see what we do with him.'

You can imagine how a statement like that made me feel.

'I'm thinking. Melanie just went to Italy. I've got a key.'

'So have I.'

'Lucky boy. In those woods you couldn't even hear a scream.'

Whose scream? Mine?

I remember, after it was all over, when I finally talked to Fiona again, she asked me, 'Did they torture you?'

'Yes,' I answered.

'Can you talk about it?'

'It's not something I like to talk about,' I said.

'You poor, dear boy.'

But I told you people I'd tell you everything, the good and the bad, so fasten your seat-belts.

I should have thrown out little scraps of paper or barleycorns, and I would have, but you can't do that while you're screeching through the countryside at seventy miles an hour, with your hands tied behind your back. I tried to keep my bearings, and remember the place names I saw on road signs. And it may well be that they were going in a roundabout way to throw me off. Anyway they did throw me off.

Finally we started through some very thick woods, and I saw one pheasant scooting out of our way, and then we pulled up at Melanie's cottage, which wasn't exactly made out of gingerbread, but made me think she must have been a witch. I mean it was very up-market gingerbread. There was a three-car garage, and we put the cars in it, next to an old MG-TD, with the top up and those isinglass curtains all around.

It was a witch's house all right. Stained glass windows, and Pre-Raphaelite pictures, people in those long droopy robes. The carpet was shaggy and hairy.

'Look,' the curly one, obviously the leader, said to me, 'you can't even go to the loo with your hands tied in the back like that.' He untied me. 'Just take off your shoes. You'd never get away in your stocking feet. You might be eaten by local cannibals, or shot by some gamekeeper as a poacher. Right?'

'Right,' I said, and gave him my shoes.

'There's a fish and chips place a couple of miles down the road, and a Macdonalds a couple of miles the other way. So we can bring the food back and stay alive.'

Did I want to stay alive?

'But what in bloody hell do we do with him until Monday?'

They sat and looked at the floor. Suddenly Curly had a gleam in his eye. I couldn't have guessed, then, how much pain that would mean for me.

'We're lucky. I remembered. There is absolutely no problem.' He turned and looked at me. I trembled.

'You like cricket?' he asked.

Before I tell you what I answered to that, let me remind you of the stories told by ordinary citizens who have been in hostage situations, like in hi-jacked planes. They told us they developed a weird feeling about their captors. They wanted to please them, to cosy up to them. Some even reported a kind of twisted love for them. Go along with it. Actually the very word cricket can make me burst into a rash. It conjures up memories of scores of Wimbledon broadcasts, when an absorbing tennis match is suddenly snatched away with the gleeful words, 'And now we go to the cricket!' Rage, rage, against the coming of the night. It won't help.

'Love it,' I said to my captor, choking on the words.

I remember what my son, Crandie, told me. He had played it at school, and became infected with the virus. 'Father,' he said, earnestly, 'you're simply incapable of understanding cricket. You were raised on baseball, which is obviously a game for working-class children, whereas cricket is a game for gentlemen. Let me try to explain it to you.' And he did try. But nothing helped.

The curly-headed stud said, 'That's rare for a Yank. Anyway you're lucky because there's a test match on. At least three more days.' He turned on the TV, and even though it was now early evening, they were still playing, had certainly been ever since morning, through lunch, and tea, heading toward night.

OK, if you haven't seen cricket, it's like this: take home plate and put it almost in the middle of the field. The other batter stands on third base, and the pitchers, lots of them, are throwing in both directions, running a fifty-yard dash before they throw the ball, which can hit the ground in front of the batter, who is protecting himself with something that looks like a canoe paddle. And he stays right there, himself, personally, sometimes hitting more than a hundred runs until he is put out, like by somebody catching a fly ball, even if it takes the whole day, from morning to night.

Imagine, if you can, just sitting there, hour after hour, watching, and watching, the monotony broken only by an occasional Big Mac or a paper cone full of fish and chips, sloshed with vinegar. I slept on the sofa, and somebody was always watching me. There was no pity anywhere.

By Monday it looked as though the Aussies were winning. The atmosphere was becoming tense. The two beautiful guys were biting their nails. The scores were into the hundreds. They looked like the Dow Jones, multiplied by ten, spread over a scoreboard as big as the side of a barn. I was wondering how long it took a healthy man to die.

Along about noon, Curly said, 'I think I'd better call Woody again.' So far he had always been talking to the robot on the answerphone. I knew that the cricket was bad enough – but that was just the antipasto. What did this Woody have in mind for the real thing?

Even from where I was sitting, I could hear the screams. Curly was visibly turning white. He tried to mutter things like, 'But I understood –'

When the call was over, Curly was shaking.

'Woody says to bring him back – right now. I've never heard him so angry.'

I couldn't get them to talk. Was somebody angry they hadn't killed me yet? They gave me my shoes and told me to put them on. In five minutes we were in the cars. Curly wasn't taking any chances. He drove me in my car – *right straight to Madeleine's.*

The very second we stopped, I opened the car door, jumped out, and ran for the house.

I almost bumped into Fiona.

'Joey, where are you going?'

'To a telephone. I'm calling the police!'

'Look at that!' she said. Curly was running to the Ferrari. He jumped in, and it roared out of the driveway.

'I think they're the ones who need the police, Joey, to protect them from Woody. Maybe I do too. The trouble is, darling, that these lovely boys were not hired for their brainpower. Woody had something else in mind. He does want to talk to you, but he was already late for his plane to Paris, and he sent me to try to explain that he can't see you for two days, and let me tell you, darling, you can simply ask him for *anything* now, and he's already planning something absolutely fabulous for you, he won't even tell me what –'

'Fifi, can you tell me what happened?'

'Well, it was partly my fault, darling. I got it all wrong because Rodney, my lover-boy, simply hates Curly, and he heard they were going to pick you up and take you to Woody; I knew Woody had just heard you were practically going to double-cross him with the man from Locksleys, the biggest casino of all, and when Woody is angry, simply anything can happen, so I assumed you were going to be kidnapped, and –'

'Fifi, somebody should spank you.'

'That's what Woody said, but he didn't have time. Would you like to, darling? You don't have to worry, Woody is planning something simply fabulous, to make it up to you, and you're going to be put on a golden platter, and taken right to him.'

'Where?'

'Venice, darling, that's where he lives.'

'Venice Italy?'

'Venice England, Jo-Jo. Haven't you noticed? Things are changing. You'll be picked up right here at Madeleine's on Wednesday, at 9 a.m., taken there. It's being arranged. She'll pick you up at Madeleine's at 9 a.m. sharp. Look for a gold-coloured Porsche. And bring your water-wings.'

'What in hell is this all about, Fifi?'

'Money, really, grampa. Woody can tell you better than I can. But if he's playing true to form you'll probably be picked up by the Girl of your Dreams whatever *she* looks like. Dress as you would for a top-drawer meeting at Rambleys.'

I realized Fifi had been right about Venice. Suddenly it has happened. London *is* becoming Venice. Everyone is thinking *water* now. And if you could see the plans, the real, approved plans, you wouldn't believe them. One, already drawn, is for a whole new Manhattan Island, but with water in between the skyscrapers down where the old London docks used to be. It will be called Canary Wharf. And many, many more. A whole fleet of catamarans, better than the *vaporetti* of Venice, is being built.

But why *now*? The River Thames has been there for centuries. Did nobody notice it? It was there, but it stank, because it was an open sewer. They used to put up wet towels in front of Parliament because the stink was so strong even the politicians couldn't stand it. Now, in the last few decades, great sewage treatment plants have been built all along the river. The water is becoming sweet, and the salmon are already returning. Now Venice is coming. And in twenty years you won't recognize London. That's where I was going, to Venice.

# *Sixteen*

At nine, sharp, wearing my second best Savile Row, I walked down Madeleine's back stairs, and there it was, a golden Porsche, not an antique, like mine, but the very latest 928. And in it was – Subby?

When she saw me coming down she stepped around to the passenger door, and opened it for me. She was a tall, cool, sexy blonde, wearing a beautiful formal suit, with a crisp white blouse. It was much too close to be accidental. She even *looked* like Subby, all but the eyes, as I could see when I got very pleasantly close. Who was behind this, Mephistopheles?

'Good morning, Sir,' she said, with a cool, sexy smile.

'Good morning, my dear. How did you know it was me?'

'I was told what you looked like, Sir.'

'Did they tell you what *you* should look like?'

'No, Sir, but they told me how to dress, and they had my hair done.'

I laughed.

'Do I look funny to you, Sir?'

'No, you look lovely, darling. Where are we going?'

'To Chelsea Harbour, Sir.'

Of course I knew about Chelsea Harbour, who didn't? P&O had taken the filthiest old tyre-retreading section of Fulham (not actually in yuppy Chelsea at all, but next to it) and had done a real Fairy Godmother treatment, spending hundreds of millions, putting in a whole yacht harbour, and scores of fancy town houses, apartment crescents, glass-domed shopping centres and a lock leading to the Thames, which flows right in front of it. They had made Belgravia, the previous Park Avenue of London, seem seem rather old and tacky, with its Rolls Royces sitting sadly in the rain. (All Chelsea Harbour's parking is underground.) And this was only one of the beginnings of Venice, England.

We drove in, near the new Conrad Hotel, and directly to the foot of the famous Belvedere, the Harbour's only skyscraper, with a little pyramid for a hat, and, on top of that, a navigation light which could tell a yachtsman, even some distance away, whether the tide was up or down. Millions of pounds worth of yachts were tied to their marina docks just beside us.

'Here we are, Sir.'

'In the Belvedere?' I had heard that each whole floor was one apartment, and they were worth more, some of them *much* more, than a million pounds each.

'Yes, Sir.' She clicked around and opened my door.

There was Security all over, very strong, but very discreet, and they had obviously been told to expect me.

A uniformed guard stepped up. 'Good morning, Sir. Come with me, please.'

We went up in the private lift. The guard had two keys, and he needed both of them to open the door. He stepped back, and said, 'Thank you, Sir.'

I was in a great room with windows on two sides, looking down on the Thames. It was furnished like a beautiful drawing-room, not like an office. The only inhabitant, a middle-aged gentleman in a business suit, rose from a padded leather swivel-chair, within reach of a computer terminal. He had a round, smiley face, and a fringe of greying hair circling a bald spot. He came to meet me.

'So good of you to come. I'm Woody Woodard.' Public school accent. 'May I call you Joseph? I know Americans always use first names.'

I grunted. A bare affirmative.

'There's no way I can apologize enough. I did hear you were talking with competitors, Locksleys, and felt I should really see you first. I made the mistake of asking our idiot pretty boys to pick you up. For some reason they got the impression you were trying to escape. I should have known that a lovely lady would suit you better. How is my lady Sublimity?'

After what I'd been through I was not amused. 'The eyes are wrong,' I said.

'Sorry about that. Didn't have time to do the tinted contacts. Can you believe she was a redhead yesterday?'

'What in blazes have you done to Fiona?'

He did really look sorry. 'I do regret that, Joseph. Truly. The name of my game – or one of my games – is gambling, of course, and to most people it's just an exciting and occasionally profitable pastime. But to some, like Fiona, it can become an addiction. I'm to blame for that. As part of our market survey I did introduce some of your influential ladies to our casinos, and did give them a little help at first.'

'You let them win?'

'We helped them not to lose. With black jack, of course, you can. But occasionally, without a helping hand, they – especially Fiona – managed to lose more than they could afford. I'm now trying to persuade her to have psychiatric help, and I'm afraid I've had to tell her our casinos are out of bounds. And as I'm sure you suspect, the only object of this exercise is to put a lovely gaming room into your Lordleigh Club, which could make it a profit of perhaps ten million pounds a year.'

'Which you would share.'

'Of course, but a very high Lordleigh profit would be guaranteed.'

'You must know that this was tried, years ago.'

'And failed completely. Lady Mountvale's very firm opinion was that it would change the whole image and character of the Club, and could even have been risky.'

'That was when Tish was president. We talked about that.' I guessed that if Woody knew Subby, down to her eye colouring, he would know all about Tish and me. 'It could have been dangerous. We might have had to deal with gangsters, even possibly the Mafia.'

'That's all changed now.'

'Are you sure?'

'Positive. There has been a complete upheaval. Gambling has now become an important industry in Britain, almost like North Sea Oil. Definitely adds to our balance of payments. So the government has put it under iron-bound rules. It is highly regulated. No one can start a casino without obtaining a license from the Gaming Board, and if the Board revokes that license there's almost no chance of its being renewed. As they say, now, only the squeaky-clean need apply. Do you know what the "drop" means?'

'No.'

'That's the amount of cash exchanged for chips. It is now running about a *billion* pounds a year, a great deal of it from your Yanks, and from Arab princes. A while back, Grand Metropolitan had six clubs up for sale at about two hundred million. We are now called the

Leisure Industry. We ourselves own hotels, restaurants, resorts, race courses, and also casinos in Mayfair, and in Europe. We have agreements with cruise ships, a place in Vegas, and another in Atlantic City. We are listed on the Stock Exchange. I know this must seem incredible to you, and of course the best way to establish credibility is – money.'

He reached down and pulled up a beautiful crocodile dispatch case and handed it to me.

'Open it, please.'

I did. It was solidly packed with bank notes, in fifty and twenty pound bills.

'It's a hundred thousand, and there is no record of it. We deal in quite a lot of cash. There are no strings on this at all. It is your present for coming to visit me, to say nothing of compensation for our unforgivable mistake. But if, together, we are able to persuade a majority of the Lordleigh debenture holders to accept the idea of a gaming room at the Club, you could become a part of our organization, not necessarily full time, you would have plenty of time to work with Max and Rambleys. Your commissions – depending upon the success of the venture – would probably come to about half a million a year. I think, with the Club's known position, at the very top of society, we might expect a drop of about a hundred million a year.

'I thought of you because you seem to have a wide acquaintance with many of the influential ladies at the Club.'

'I play a lot of mixed doubles.'

'Good game, isn't it?' I thought I detected a wink. 'You might help us to think about ways we could work this out. It could be done with as much protection for the Club as you would want, even a limited trial period, the limit to be set by you, as well as the hours of opening. Perhaps only after 10 p.m. Perhaps with a separate entrance. And perhaps, if we both wanted to maximize the income, there might be separate memberships, valid only after opening time, and only for the gaming room, at gaming times. That might allow certain selected people – selected subject to your veto, of course – like certain known high-rolling Americans, or members of the Arabian aristocracy. I have already made discreet enquiries, and I think we would be successful in obtaining a licence from the Gaming Board, and planning permission from your local council.'

There is something about having a hundred thousand pounds in your lap that tends to make you speechless.

'Of course you'll want time to think about this, and perhaps to talk with some of your friends.'

'Yes,' I said.

'The car is only leased for the day, but if you became a member of our organization, perhaps you'd like to turn in your car for a new one.'

'That would be nice.'

'We might even be able to provide a driver – of your choice, of course. Do you have any questions, Joseph?'

'I'll probably think of some, Woody.'

'We'll send the car for you again. Thank you so much for coming.'

He gave me his most sincere, squeaky-clean smile, and escorted me personally to the lift.

The golden car and the Subby clone were waiting for me.

'Where would you like to go now, Sir? I'm at your service the rest of the day, if you wish.'

As we moved away from the yachts, I could see that her skirt was pulled up, but discreetly, above her knees, and that her legs were almost as good as Gwenny's, or Tish's. She certainly must have been at the very top of her profession.

'Everything is already paid for, Sir.' She gave me a very cool, but very sexy smile. '*Everything*.'

'And you're very lovely, darling. I *do* wish I had time. Actually I prefer red-headed ladies.'

She laughed.

'I'll take a rain-check, my dear.'

'What's a rain-check, Sir?'

'It's American for *mañana*. Tomorrow, darling. I'd better go back to Lady Richey's now, please.'

# *Seventeen*

I phoned Lulu at her rain forest, and told her I had some things to say that I'd better say in person.

'It's always better in person, Joey,' she said. I drove right out. She brought me into her jungle-under-glass, beside a banana tree, with wraparound leaves.

'Are you all right, luv?' I said. Her eyes looked red. 'Have you been crying?'

'It's nothing, Joey. Something I was reading. One of my Vassar friends sent it to me, written by a man I once knew, named Mongane Serote, a black man. For a while he studied at Columbia, in New York, and I heard him read some of his poetry. It was like singing. This novel of his I was reading is called *To Every Birth Its Blood*. He once lived and worked in Alexandra township, near Johannesburg, where he said his poetry was bursting at its seams, and where he felt the sky was an empty hole. A brilliant man, a strange novel. I guess it just brought out the black in me, Joey.'

I told her all that Woody had told me, and she thought about it for quite a while. 'Well, maybe it's the black in me that Mongane brought out, but I think this thing would be bad for the club. You know people are just as important as animals, Joey.'

'That's a big concession from you, mate.'

'Sometimes they're mistreated even more than animals, aren't they? In some ways this Woody thing seems to me like people-pollution. I don't think he's really wicked, or that gambling is all that bad, though it must have been bad for Fiona. I'd bet it could be bad for some of the others. Loadsa money, sure. But do we need it that much? What does Tish think about it?'

'I'll let you know, Lulu. I have a date to see her tomorrow.'

Tish met me at the door to her tennis building, and gave me a nice, slightly lingering but just friendly kiss.

'I want to hear it all, Joey, but first I'm going to beat your socks off in at least two sets, and then I'm going to have a nice swim with you, and if you even *touch* me, I'll scream.'

'So who needs to touch you? Remember?'

'Damn you, Jo-Jo!' But with a smile.

'I intend to spank you anyway, Tishia, so I'll have to touch you.'

We split sets. I blame that on the surface, *her* surface, much more familiar to her, and better suited to her game.

In the pool she was wearing a different, and even more skin-tight golden lycra swimsuit. This required superhuman character on my part, but my character is growing all the time now, and we both kept our bathing costumes on. We showered separately. Sort of a tacit agreement. We both knew that character could stretch only so far.

And then we went, not to the bedrom, but to the great library, and sat between one of the Turners and a Lautrec. Nancy brought us a tea as big as a banquet. This time she did look at me, and gave me just a trace of a smile. I smiled, and nodded, but nothing more.

'Will that be all Milady?'

'Yes, Nancy, thank you.'

I told Tish the whole Woody thing.

'So you see,' I said, 'at least a casino is a good deal safer this time than it was before.'

'Yes, I agree. But I always thought we could handle the Mafia part. I'd have had them bring in the SAS if necessary. Two things. If we did decide to do it, why should we share the gravy with this Woody? I know people on the Gaming Board. I could get us a license to gamble, and planning permission, and we could hire a top manager, but one we could control, and keep a firm hold on the reins. Sack him if necessary. But I still have the same objection. It would change the quality of the Club, for the worse. We don't need it, and we don't need the money that much. Now you can tell me Louisa's reaction. And about the water buffaloes.'

'Lulu agrees with you. But she's still determined to keep the Club green. She's going to call you, and the other ladies. The problem now is butterflies, not buffaloes. They don't like the insecticide spray we're using.'

'Well, who does? By the way, Joey, I'm looking for a partner in the new Big Mixed.'

'I'll see if I can find somebody who can stand you, baby.' I gave her a bit of a squeeze. 'Actually I signed us up – subject to your approval.'

'Thank you, Joey.'

'So I'm now your Official Outdoor Boy?'

'As long as you behave yourself, darling. Just don't let me catch you coming indoors. Unless I ring for you, of course.'

I talked to Jamie and Joanna and Mabel. We agreed that the gaming room, on our own terms, was a possibility. We could do it if we wanted, and if we had an urgent need for money. For the moment, we thought the Club would be better without it.

I visited Woody in Chelsea Harbour. I always say, don't ever slam any expensive doors. You never know, do you? I said, not for now, right now, but don't go away. And I gave him back the money.

'Are you surprised?'

'No, not really, Joseph. I rather expected you would, if you couldn't bring it off. You know where to find me, and I know where to find you. My little girl has gone back to being a redhead. You did disappoint her, Joseph. I think she rather fancied you. And, I might add, you don't know how much you missed. She told me she still owes you one. All you need to do is whistle.'

He gave me his squeaky-clean smile, and escorted me out.

I knew that Subby was having another bad weekend, nourishing and playing amateur-shrink for a wandering American genius. She said on the phone he'd actually had a wife with him.

So on Sunday afternoon I was able to park near her house, and let myself in. I was a few minutes later than usual, and she was already out of her shower. But she came running to me in her white terry cloth robe, and flung it open to join me.

'Oh, Joey, Joey, don't say a word, the cover is off the bed, and I'm simply starving for you.'

After that, I told her everything. The Subby-clone part made her laugh.

'I must say I'm proud of you, Joey. You just had close encounters with both Tish and Lulu. And I can tell, lover-boy, that you're still a boy scout.'

'Character, luv, you gotta have character. Will you marry me now, Subby?'

'Let's not overdo it, Mono-Joe. Who knows, I might want to try out a younger fella. You're not a kid any more.'

But she kissed me sweetly, and gave me a squeeze.